HUMANE SACRIFICE

The Story of the Aztec Killer

BY FELIX I.D. DIMARO

HUMANE SACRIFICE

The Story of the Aztec Killer

Written by FELIX I.D. DIMARO

Cover Artwork and Interior Artwork: Rosco Nischler
Typography: Courtney Swank
Editing: Ally Sztrimbely

ALSO BY FELIX I.D. DIMARO

How To Make A Monster: The Loveliest Shade of Red

Bug Spray: A Tale of Madness

Viral Lives: A Ghost Story

2222

The Fire On Memory Lane

The Corruption of Philip Toles

Black Bloom: A Story of Survival

Us In Pieces: Stories of Shattered Souls

Warning

This story contains mature content, including explicit and derogatory language, adult themes, scenes depicting graphic violence, and a great deal of blood.

Discretion is advised.

For Cat. I'm sure you still can't read, even from beyond the grave, but I know you knew how much you meant to me. Thank you for this story.

"If having a soul means being able to feel love and loyalty and gratitude, then animals are better off than a lot of humans."

– James Herriot

"In ancient times cats were worshipped as gods; they have not forgotten this."

– Terry Pratchett

1

"You're wrong!" Melvin Cockburn shouted, shaking his head from side to side, refusing to acknowledge the information he had been given. Despite this not being the first time he had been told this bitter piece of news, he was unwilling to accept the diagnosis, the prognosis; he was unwilling to accept the situation at all. "You're wrong! That lazy prick of a vet is wrong! You just don't want to help!"

"Mr. *Cock*burn, I assure you, we have done our best to help Lucy. But, as we've told you for weeks now, there is *nothing* that can be done to save her. The humane thing to do, as someone who cares about her, is to let her go peacefully." Standing behind the reception area desk, using it as a protective barrier between herself and Melvin, the veterinary assistant looked from Melvin's face to his hand. To the pet carrier he held in it. At Lucy, his cat, who lay dying inside of the carrier.

If Melvin didn't know better, he would have believed the sad expression on the vet assistant's face. He would have believed she cared. "And do it soon, Mr. *Cock*burn. She's in rough shape. Now, please, I would appreciate it if you would keep your voice down. You're not doing Lucy any favours."

"It's pronounced *Co*-burn. Cooo-burn! And you *know* that!" He hated when people did that – mispronounced his name, teased him. People had been making fun of his name since he was a child. "Don't you fucking tell me how to take care of my cat!" Melvin roared into the reception area of the South Saturn Animal Hospital, the place he had been taking Lucy to for years now. A place he regretted bringing her to in the first place.

He needed a second opinion, that's what he needed. A second opinion from someone who wasn't intent on murdering his best friend. What he didn't need was any more lip from some ditzy, glorified secretary.

The tall, thin woman standing across from him sighed. Blew out a frustrated breath that sent her frizzy brown bangs flying from her forehead. She looked toward the phone on the desk in front of her as if considering using it. He could see what was on her mind. 911. The police. She would lie and tell them he was a threat. Some sort of danger to her safety. But all he wanted was to be listened to. All he wanted was for someone to try to save his cat.

"Sir. I'm going to have to ask you to leave. You're frightening the animals, and you're making everyone uncomfortable."

He opened his mouth to rebuke her. To tell her, the two old ladies sitting there in the reception area watching him, and their little beagle, to all go fuck themselves. But then he heard Lucy mewling. He must have jostled her. As much as he hated to admit it, the vet assistant was right. Lucy sounded frightened.

"You're a murderer," Melvin said in a harsh whisper, leaning over the desk, breathing into her face. "This is a goddamn butcher shop."

He trudged away, feeling six pairs of human eyes and one pair of beagle eyes on him as he walked the short distance from the desk to the door, then out of it, as Lucy meowed despondently all the while.

2

Melvin was fuming as he walked outside into the late summer air. It was a lovely early September afternoon. Or at least it should have been. It was sunny and warm, the sky was cloudless and clear. But he didn't feel the warmth. The world to him was grey and gloomy. It had been that way since the vet had begun talking about killing his little Lucy two months ago; when the golf ball sized tumour on her chest had become too hard to ignore. The hair covering it had fallen off, leaving the area pink and angry and portending the pain that would be her future. And his.

Now it was much worse. The tumour had grown, opened up, become infected. It was a baseball sized pustule, malodorous and ever leaking. Draining her, stealing her away.

It shouldn't have gotten this bad, Melvin believed. Lucy shouldn't have become this sick. He had implored the vet to help, begged him for a solution. And what had that charlatan of an animal doctor done in response to Melvin's desperate pleas? Dr. Antoine Torsten had tried to gouge him for nearly fifteen hundred dollars in exchange for simply removing the lump.

Melvin didn't have that kind of money. He barely had money for food. When he couldn't pay up on the vet's ransom, Dr. Torsten had gone straight to torture and death, making Melvin watch his best pal suffer until it was time to 'let her go,' as Dr. Torsten and his obnoxious assistant had stated it. Melvin felt he had been given no options between being extorted and watching his cat slowly dying.

"Criminals," Melvin muttered to himself. "Murderers and criminals!"

He had only taken a few steps from the animal hospital when he stopped. Hatred held him back, rage made it so he couldn't bring himself to walk away. Instead, he gently placed Lucy's carrier down on the curb before turning back to the building, grumbling as he did so.

"That goddamn butcher of a vet. That fucking criminal and his stupid flat chested, air headed, mealy-mouthed bitch of an assistant..."

He hadn't known what to say before he had walked out, but he knew what he would say now. He was going to make sure that snotty assistant heard it. And the veterinarian, too.

"Give those motherfuckers a piece of my mi–"

He stopped a few feet from the door. Someone was in front of it. A figure was blocking his entry.

It was someone who hadn't been there before. And Melvin couldn't remember seeing this person in the lobby of the animal hospital only moments prior.

How did he get there so fast? Melvin wondered, considering the few steps he had taken from the building, knowing that only seconds had passed since he had been in the same spot this person was standing in now.

It was a well-dressed man.

He wore a red blazer over black pants and a black collared shirt. Keeping the collar of that shirt together was a red and black bowtie. On his head was a black fedora, a bright red feather jutting from its side. Melvin looked at the feather and blinked. In the light of the sun, it appeared as though it was on fire.

The man only stared. A pale pink lipped smile that was illogically wide spread across a face that had features which seemed to melt into each other. A face of no distinction.

The smile disturbed Melvin, but it was this stranger's eyes that truly startled the disgruntled pet owner. They

4

were the bluest eyes Melvin had ever seen. From behind a pair of glasses with thick red frames, they shone into the day like plasma balls. Like electricity trapped in glass globes wanting to burst free.

He was an unsettling man to look upon.

As Melvin stared at this stranger, he realized that he'd had his say. He was no longer in the mind of speaking to the assistant at the front desk. Not if it meant having to interact with this person blocking his path.

Feeling defeated, helpless, Melvin picked Lucy's carrier up. Her soft whimpering was like a hand closing on his intestines, squeezing, twisting, making his hatred for everyone in the building he had been kicked out of grow. He swallowed that hate now, and it made his stomach knot up further.

Head down, shoulders slumped, feet dragging, Melvin carried Lucy to the bus stop. The entire way there, he could sense the strange man watching him. Staring at him. He could feel those too-blue eyes inside of that unsettling face boring into his back. Into his soul.

3

"It'll be okay, little Lucy. We'll be home soon," Melvin said in response to his cat whimpering from her carrier. He was walking from the bus stop to his home on the east side of Saturn City, a mid-sized city neighbouring Toronto. His was a small, old, two storey house near the top of a crescent in the lower-middle class neighbourhood of Verndale. Well, it was not his house, technically. It was his mother's home. It was her name alone on the deed. The only official documents including Melvin's name were those in which he was listed as the adult dependent of Moira Cockburn. He lived in her basement, as he had his entire life. He loathed the place he lived and was never in a rush to get there.

Melvin was walking slowly, rigidly, careful not to rattle Lucy in her carrier. He had made it nearly all the way home that way until he stumbled on the uneven sidewalk across the road from his house and shook the sick cat badly.

Cursing at himself, Melvin placed the carrier on the ground to check on his best friend. To apologize and let her know they were only seconds away from home. He felt terrible in that moment seeing Lucy's obvious dismay. He was made to feel worse when he heard the voices emerging from the porch of the house across from his. The house he was kneeling in front of while talking into Lucy's carrier.

"Is he having a conversation with his cat?" one voice, a woman's, said.

Titters. Chuckles.

"What a fucking loser," a male voice responded.

Chortles. Laughs.

He stood carefully, the carrier in his hand. He didn't bother to look to his left where he knew he would see the neighbours who lived across the street from him, a young married couple, Mr. and Mrs. Gorman.

They were a pair of perpetually inebriated hippies who spent much of their warm-weather days wearing too little, showing off their bodies while on the front porch drinking, or in the backyard drinking, or having boisterous parties with their hippy friends, all of them drinking too.

All the time, they played their music too loudly. All the time, they were too loud in general. And they were mean, at least to Melvin. It wasn't enough that they were young, good looking, cool, and had each other. They had to rub it in his face that he was none of those things. That he had no one.

He hated walking past their house. Hated them. They acted as his personal commentators whenever they saw him striding by. They often let out drunken whispers which were practically shouts to the sober. And he heard them every time. 'Fucking loser' was the insult they liked most.

Their laughter followed him as he crossed the road and approached his house. Walked up the pair of steps onto the landing that made up the rundown porch (which was much smaller and in far worse condition than the Gormans').

He took a deep breath before reaching into his pocket for his key. And prepared himself for the hostility that awaited him on the other side of the door.

4

"That you, Melly?" a sharp and grating voice called down the stairs to him the moment he had opened the door. It was like pins pricking at his eardrums.

Who the fuck else would it be? he thought darkly. Aloud, he said,

"Yes, it's me, mom!"

He hated when she called him Melly. Hated when anyone called him that name. The kids in elementary school had called him Smelly Melly for years. Then, when they had realized the provocative nature of the spelling of his surname, they had added that to the rhyming insult as well. And he went from Melvin Cockburn to Smelly Melly Cockburn to Smelly Smelly Cock-sperm.

Kids, they're assholes.

"Jesus, you ain't put that cat down yet?" Moira Cockburn called down to her only child from the landing at the top of the stairs. She had emerged from her room moving faster than her eighty-year-old frame ought to have carried her. Melvin looked at his mother, her thinning white hair a mess upon her head. She was dressed in one of her usual outfits, a plush robe the colour of pale peaches. And she was wearing one of her many pairs of oversized fluffy novelty slippers. Her feet were currently inside of a couple of faded red rabbit heads. They were supposed to be cute, but to Melvin they were morbid.

Moira Cockburn was old, but she had never appeared feeble. Not even after having to replace a hip a few years back. Every time he saw her, he checked for signs that she was weakening, finally wearing down, but she always seemed as strong as ever. He wondered, looking at her now, if she would live forever. And shivered at the thought.

"Christ! I can smell that goddamn thing from here!"

"That 'goddamn thing' has a name, and it's *Lucy*! And she's sick, *mom!*"

Despite her thinning white hair, Moira Cockburn looked younger than her eighty years. She was medium height, and thickly built, which was something she had been sensitive about for as long as Melvin could remember. She had often told him when he was a child that she'd once had the figure of a model. But then he had come along and turned her body to ruins. He couldn't help but look at her when she said that, an up and down evaluation each time. Checking for signs of the 'ruins' he had made of her. To him, she had always looked like most other moms. Apparently that hadn't been good enough for her. As a child he had grown to understand, slowly and painfully, learning harsh lessons that were part of a lifelong curriculum of pain and maternal cruelty, that he hadn't been good enough for her either. And never would be.

He was the child she had never planned for. He was her unwanted spawn. And she never failed to remind him of that.

Now, after forty-two years of listening to his mother's meanness, his resentment had grown to match hers. And their mutual disdain for one another seemed to increase each day.

"Sick? You sure it ain't dead? Sure smells like it's dead." Moira said from the top of the staircase. Melvin was about to reply, to defend his smelly little sidekick, but his mother cut him off before he could get a word in. "Just keep that thing where I can't smell it!"

She turned from the landing and went back to her room, slamming the door behind her as she always did. He could hear her shuffle to her bed in her stupid slippers and climb atop it as she went for her daily nap.

Melvin stood there, seething, one foot on the first step, the other on the first floor, not sure what to do. He wanted to go up the steps and follow his mother; continue this screaming match, vent his frustrations. Melvin wanted to make sure she didn't get the last word as she always did. He was also considering stepping down from the riser, taking Lucy and retreating to his basement as he always did; ignoring his mother as he had tried to do all his life. He could spend the rest of the day watching television with Lucy. That would be the peaceful alternative.

Fight or flight, neither choice felt fruitful. As he stood there frozen and frowning, the decision was made for him in the form of a third, unexpected option.

The doorbell rang.

The sound, so foreign and unexpected in this house, and during this tense moment, caused Melvin to jump and somehow nearly fall down the single step he was half stood upon.

He turned toward the door he had recently entered and briefly wondered who it could be before deciding not to answer. It didn't matter who it was, he thought. Neither he nor his mother had any friends. The only people who rang on his doorbell were the twerpy little college kid who had previously lived down the street and was still paid (too much, in Melvin's opinion) to do the grocery shopping and snow shovelling for Moira, and the Jehovah's Witnesses who had been trying to convert his mother for at least a decade.

No one came by to visit Melvin.

If it was either of his mother's usual visitors, she would have been expecting them, welcoming them, not in bed sleeping.

"Just some stupid solicitor," Melvin whispered under his breath, as if worried the person on the other side of the door might hear him and become aware that they were being ignored. Melvin turned from the door. With

Lucy's carrier in hand, he was about to make his way downstairs to his lair when the doorbell rang again.

He paused but didn't turn to answer it. Decided to continue on his path. He walked down the hallway, reached the basement door, and put his hand on the knob. That's when the person at the door began to ring relentlessly.

It was a desperate sort of ringing. No space between sounds, no pause for those inside the home to respond to this unexpected caller. The sound of it was frenzied, like there was some sort of emergency nearby, and Melvin was needed to respond. He wondered briefly if that might be the case – a disaster in the neighbourhood someone was hoping to alert him or his mother about.

Not my problem, Melvin told himself glumly, recalling how awful some of his neighbours were. *Maybe a disaster is exactly what they deserve.*

It would be his problem, however, if the incessant ringing wound up disturbing his mother. She would be angry and somehow find a way to blame him. Arguing with a cranky, pissed off Moira Cockburn after her nap had been interrupted was not something high on the list of things he ever wanted to do. Still, he considered letting that happen. Letting the visitor keep ringing the doorbell until his mother had to limp her way down the stairs and became enraged because of it. That would serve her right for saying all she had said. Not just today, for his entire life.

But then Lucy made a noise. A growl deep in her belly. The sound she made right before she was about to hiss.

It was Melvin who now became enraged by the caller at the door, because this unwanted visitor had upset his little girl.

He set Lucy's carrier down in front of the basement door before spinning on his socked heels on the tiled floor and turning toward the entrance. Melvin marched more so than walked to the front door as the person on the other side of it continued to ring madly on the bell.

5

Melvin reached the front door, twisted the lock viciously, and wrenched the door open even as the ringing bell continued to sound in his ears.

His mouth was open before the door was. His sentence was started before he could see who he was shouting at.

"Hey! What the fuck is the big deal? My cat is trying to rest! This better be..." His words were cut short by what he saw. It was as though someone had taken his larynx in their grip and squeezed. Because what he saw when he opened his door not only made him suddenly short of words, but also short of breath.

The ringing had stopped as soon as the door was opened. Logically, there should have been someone immediately in front of him, their hand outstretched in the direction of the doorbell. Logically.

But, illogically, the person was five feet away from him, standing there calmly on his walkway, feet firmly planted before the two steps that would lead to the small porch, hands by their sides, even as the echo of the last chime of the bell rang through the foyer behind Melvin.

The inconsistency of what he had heard and what he now saw caused him to twitch, caused him to feel disoriented.

It wasn't only the distance of this stranger from the door that made Melvin feel disturbed, it was also the person themself.

It was somebody he recognized.

In front of Melvin, on his walkway, was the same well dressed but unsettling man who had been standing outside of the animal hospital.

"Hello, Mr. Cockburn," the familiar stranger said, seemingly emphasizing the correct pronunciation of the surname for Melvin's benefit.

"Can I... Can I help you?" Melvin asked meekly, his discomfort, his bewilderment, his fear once again causing his rage to dissipate.

Melvin was looking at a man out of time. The bright blazer, the bowtie, the red framed glasses, the fedora, the odd red feather that stuck out of that lid; it all seemed to belong to some long ago decade. In addition to his anachronistic clothes, the man carried a large, ancient looking satchel of a briefcase that hinted to Melvin what this person was. An antiquated look for an antiquated profession.

This person appeared, altogether, as though he had stepped out of the past from a bygone era. And when he opened his mouth, Melvin wasn't surprised to hear that the stranger's voice, both in tone and timber, reminded him of a recording of an old sports broadcast. Like how a baseball announcer from back in the sixties, or maybe the fifties or earlier, might sound. Old-timey was the way the voice translated to Melvin's mind. But its old-fashioned quality wasn't the oddest aspect of this man's voice. To Melvin's surprise, the sounds the stranger made didn't match the movement of his lips. He spoke, his lips made the appropriate shapes to match his words, but they were disconnected. His words and his mouth, they were somehow out of a sync, like a poorly dubbed video.

"I was actually wondering if *you* would allow *me* to help *you*, Mr. Cockburn. You *and* your little Lucy," this door-to-door salesman – this Pitchman – said. He appeared to take joy in Melvin's obvious surprise at hearing his and his cat's names emerge from that unnervingly wide mouth.

Smiling his too-large smile, his too-many-toothed grin, he momentarily stared past Melvin and focused his brilliant blue gaze on Lucy in her carrier by the basement door before turning those eyes back to Melvin and continuing his spiel. He lifted his attaché to chest level, showing it to Melvin as though it contained all the answers to every question in the world. Then, in his outmoded, out of sync way of speaking, The Pitchman said,

"Can I interest you in better days?"

6

They were in the basement.

Melvin didn't remember how he had gotten down there. Not specifically. Not the hallway, not the steps. Didn't recall sitting down as this stranger made a presentation stage of his little living area.

What he remembered was being nearly mesmerized by the eyes of the man who had shown up unexpectedly at his door. He remembered being asked a question and responding with his own.

"How? How can you make my days better?"

The Pitchman had continued smiling. Holding his large satchel in front of him, showing to Melvin the logo that was pressed on its side, he answered the question of a question with yet another question.

"May I come in?"

Melvin had said yes.

And now they were in the basement, and Melvin had never felt more self-conscious. It was rare for him to have a visitor. On occasion, some repairman would come to look at the furnace or tinker with the water heater. But in terms of having someone in his personal space, sharing it with him, it hadn't happened in decades. Not since early on in high school. Not since the last time he'd had a friend other than Lucy.

Looking around at the unfinished basement of his mother's house, seeing it through the eyes of someone else, some professional, he felt embarrassed. The place looked like the room of a child, mainly because it had been. He had moved down here at age twelve, and it hadn't changed much since.

In what passed for a den, there was the coffee table made of battered, peeling, faded wood he had found on the curb in front of someone's house, placed there to be collected with the trash, back in the eighth grade. His Magnavox television with its old-fashioned rabbit ear antennas was nearly as outdated as the clothing of the man with Melvin in the basement. It was supposed to play in colour but mostly played in black and white, or sometimes green. The small area rug under the coffee table and over the concrete floor was nearly as old as he was. It was faded, threadbare.

On the walls – duct taped to them because nails and tacks would not penetrate concrete – were posters. Some from his youth, some he had added more recently: The Incredible Hulk, Thor, Spiderman. Along with those heroes were his heroes from the sporting world: Tim Horton, Börje Salming, and Felix Potvin of the Toronto Maple Leafs, Joe Carter and Rance Mullunix of the Toronto Blue Jays, and Jim Kelly of the Buffalo Bills. Posted up along with those were women he admired (mostly with his penis): Pamela Anderson, Heather Lochlear, Farrah Fawcett, Halle Berry, Cindy Crawford, Suzanne Somers. It was a shrine to things he could never be and all he could never attain.

Behind his worn recliner and ratty couch was a curtain separating the living area from the twin bed and mirrorless dresser he considered a bedroom. On the far side of the basement was another curtain, beyond which was the laundry room.

He had no separate entrance, no kitchen or bathroom of his own. His mother came down once a week to do the laundry. He went upstairs only when he had to shit or shower – though he typically just washed his important parts while standing over the laundry room sink. When he had to urinate, he did so in the sink as well. He washed his few dishes in that same laundry basin.

He kept a hotplate, a deep freezer he shared with his mother that was full of frozen dinners, a microwave, and

17

a mini fridge. All so he wouldn't have to run into his mom upstairs. He tried to avoid her as much as he could, especially when she was in the kitchen. Particularly when she was into her wine. He avoided her the way he wished he could have avoided this salesman who was standing there smiling at him with a mouth that would have looked more fitting on a shark, an alligator, a creature with too many teeth inside its head.

Melvin reassessed his décor and his life while sitting on his faded brown leather recliner which was patched in places with silver duct tape. The chair was where he spent most of his time while in front of that old and dying television, escaping reality with his cat sitting on his lap. That had been back when she was healthy. More recently, Lucy would spend her time on a towel on the floor beside the recliner, not having the energy to leap up onto him the way she always had. And she refused to let him lift her onto him, hissing violently and even scratching and biting him if he attempted to carry her, the discomfort from the tumour on her chest being far too great for her to tolerate his touch for long.

That tumour was currently covered up by two maxi pads to absorb the blood, the pus, the ooze that constantly secreted from it. Those two maxi pads were secured to and covered by a onesie which Lucy hated to wear. But those pads and that article of clothing had done much to extend Lucy's life, to help battle or at least diminish the infections which constantly found themselves in her tumour. Infections that the vet charged him an arm and a leg to treat with a simple shot each month since having declared Lucy terminal.

Would that be what was in this stranger's briefcase? More medicine that would only offer temporary relief? Vials and syringes full of false hope. Pills and potions made of empty promises.

At the moment, Lucy didn't seem to have the energy to so much as crawl out of her carrier despite the door being open. Melvin had set her down on the floor near the recliner, attempted to coax her from her carrier. She had only lain there, unmoving, uninterested. He had tried to rouse her for nearly a minute before quitting and sitting, the failure making him more open to hearing this strange man's spiel.

"It doesn't always have to be this way, you know?" The Pitchman said in his old-timey almost sing-song way of speaking. He was standing in the center of the living area, his presence there – his pristine attire, his perfect posture, his fancy hat with its red feather – making the space look smaller, more cluttered, more pathetic than it already was. Melvin had rarely felt less adequate about simply existing in the presence of someone else. His guest gestured to Lucy in the carrier on the floor beside Melvin's chair.

"She could truly live again if that is what you require."

The Pitchman had been carrying his briefcase the entire time they had been inside the house. Now he went to set it down on Melvin's cluttered table, something that would not be easy to do. On the table were remote controls, piles of paper, dirty plates, and partially filled cups of old juice, spoiled milk, and flat pop.

Ashamed of the mess that was his life, Melvin was about to approach the table to clear a spot for the man's baggage. But, to his surprise, when The Pitchman went to place his case on the table, there was a clear patch of worn brown wood exactly the size of the attaché that Melvin was certain hadn't been there a blink before. It was as if the items on the table had slid and shifted out of the way of their own accord. Melvin had to blink several times more before he found himself staring unblinkingly, telling himself that he had not just seen what he had seen. That it was a trick of the light that had made it appear as though the papers, plates, fast food bags and containers on the table had moved to make room for this man's attaché.

The case landed on the table with a substantial thud, as though it weighed a hundred pounds or more. Melvin wondered how the man had been able to carry it for so long with so little effort. Once again, his eyes were drawn to the logo on the side of it.

He wondered just what this company he had never heard of would enable this man to say on its behalf. What pitch he might make to attempt to pry the little bit of money from Melvin's nearly empty wallet.

Melvin looked from the man to his cat's carrier, at Lucy who didn't have the strength to make use of the open door. How could this person fix Lucy when the vet said nothing could be done. Nothing that wouldn't cost Melvin thousands of dollars.

Was this man trying to do the same thing? Did he have what equated to snake oil in that case of his? Had he heard Melvin's pain while at the animal clinic and followed him home in an attempt to bilk him? To swindle him out of money he clearly didn't have.

"Look... sir. You're wasting your time if you're hoping to sell me something. I know I said you could come in..." Why? Why had he said this peculiar stranger could enter his house? He had been desperate, that's why. But now his discomfort was outweighing his desperation, and he wanted this sales pitch to be over with. "But I don't have any money. As you can see, I'm not exactly living a life of luxury here."

"I require none of your money, nor your possessions, Mr. Cockburn. I simply want to help a poor animal in need, and the man who clearly, desperately, loves her. For that, all I require is your time."

"They said it was impossible. That it's too late for Lucy," Melvin responded. His voice sounded flat to his own ears, slow, drawn out, as though he were half asleep, or freshly roused from it. This was the effect of the man's voice, he realized. It was hypnotizing him, calming him, each sound he spoke a sedative.

"Is it?" The Pitchman asked. Melvin flinched as his guest moved from his spot by the table and walked the short distance to the cat carrier. He stooped down, held out a hand, snapped the fingers of that hand.

"It's no use. I've tri–" Melvin began to declare. But to his surprise (and bitter envy), from the carrier emerged his little orange Tabby cat. And she looked even worse than she had when he had put her in it.

7

Lucy looked frail, emaciated. Her once full coat of vibrant orange fur was now fading to yellow, thinning, patchy in places. She was dragging her back legs behind her, causing him to think of a person spilled from their wheelchair, desperate to return to it. Watching her move was heartbreak, but seeing her finally respond, despite his jealousy, gave him a bit of hope in the man in his basement. It made him want to believe.

"'Too late,' 'no use.' Such negativity, Mr. Cockburn. What I need you to do is have faith. Take heart." Lucy was now purring as she sniffed the stranger's fingers. "A creature that inspires this much devotion from its owner must make for a mighty fine pet. She reminds me of my own long gone little friend, sweet thing."

"Your cat... died?"

"As most things do!" The Pitchman said, turning from the cat to its owner. "But not dear Lucy! At least not yet."

"How?" Melvin asked dumbly, staring at his cat who was half the size she had been just months ago. She had deteriorated so quickly. He felt that neither of them had gotten a chance to accept what was happening. But now, somehow, if this man was telling the truth, what was happening didn't have to happen.

The Pitchman stood erect, looked from Lucy to Melvin. With the movement of his head, his body, so too moved the room. That's what it felt like to Melvin. The walls appeared to waver, the air itself seemed to vibrate around the man. The temperature increased.

"Your time, Mr. Cockburn. I require it."

His voice came from his mouth, but also from all around the room. From the speakers of the stereo, from the television that was now on, showing static when it had been dark a moment before. His voice was coming from the vents. To Melvin's ears, it sounded like this man was omnipresent. Like he was in front of him yet everywhere.

On the floor, now laying on her side, her head upside down, staring at her owner, Lucy began to meow impatiently.

"Your time." Then The Pitchman held out his hand and took a few steps closer to Melvin. The motion of his hand, his body, sent a hot gust of wind in Melvin's direction. It felt like he had stuck his face directly in front of an air vent cranked to its highest setting. The Pitchman smelled, vaguely, like something that had been set on fire.

"But I don't understand," Melvin said, his face burning, his voice still lethargic though now full of fear. What was it that was being asked of him? He shifted uncomfortably in his seat, away from this unsettling man and his demanding hand.

And that was when he felt it.

Something on his seat that hadn't been there before, something hard and warm pressed against the small of his back. He flinched yet again, nearly leaping out of his recliner. Composing himself as Lucy continued her incessant meowing, he reached behind his back and grabbed the object he was pressed against. Brought it out in front of him.

When he saw it, he gasped.

It was an object he had never seen before. One that should not, could not, have been there on his seat. But it had been. Now it was in his hand, and he knew this was what The Pitchman wanted.

The thing he held was the size of one of the pop cans on the table. It was made of black stone with runnels of red running through it. Like volcanic ash and magma caught, cooled, and crafted. Where it wasn't stone, it was glass. Glass blown and shaped into a figure eight, bulbous on the top and bottom, tapering from both ends until the rounded portions met at a thin point in the middle. Inside of that glass was blue sand.

In Melvin's hand, he held an hourglass. A Timepiece. And it was already running low.

It grew hotter, throbbing in his hand, pulsating rapidly in tune with his heart. It was disquieting. And he wanted it away from him.

He gave it over to The Pitchman, who received it with a widening of that ever-present smile.

The Pitchman walked back to his briefcase. Leaned over, opened it. And Melvin was able to see why it was so heavy.

There were dozens of hourglasses in that attaché of his, a hundred, perhaps more. Far too many to fit into the case he was carrying. Yet there they all were.

How many people had he helped?

How many had he provided with better days in exchange for their time?

Melvin was curious but couldn't be bothered to ask. He had paid his price and now wanted to know what he had purchased.

"My cat. How can you save her?" he asked anxiously, leaning forward to look at The Pitchman as he closed his case.

"It's simple," The Pitchman said, his hands remaining on the latches of his attaché. He opened it again, causing Melvin to gasp. His stomach clenched, and he nearly turned his briefs into a diaper.

The case was empty. Empty except for one item. One item that moved upon the case's blue velvet lining.

It was a mouse.

A small white mouse. Like something one would find in a science lab. Like something purchased from a pet store. Not to be made a pet but to be made into pet food.

"If you want your cat to live," said The Pitchman, grabbing the mouse by the tail before it could scurry out of the case, "you have to feed her life."

He walked toward Lucy with the mouse still squirming in his hand. He dropped it in front of the cat. Lucy reached for it, but was too weak, not fast enough. The mouse sprinted away, running under the door dividing Melvin's space from the stairwell leading upstairs.

"Fuck," Melvin said, his voice slow and hazy, the world around him the same. Everything was slowed except The Pitchman, who was moving rapidly back toward his attaché.

"My mom is gonna kill me if she sees that mouse."

As if on cue, there was a scream from upstairs. Followed by:

"A rat! A rat! A goddamn rat!"

The Pitchman chuckled, a titter that seemed to bounce against the walls and bombard the panicking Melvin.

"Remember, Mr. Cockburn, you have to feed her *life*," he said, closing his attaché before immediately opening it again.

This time the single item inside of it was familiar but foreign to Melvin. It was a doorknob. But one unlike any he had ever seen. Like the Timepiece, it was jet-black and red-veined. And, like the Timepiece, it was designed to resemble a figure eight. It contained three shining red gems inside of it – two in the top half of the eight, and one in the bottom, each shaped like a star. The gems reflected the light in the room, dazzling Melvin as they glowed, entrancing him further than he already was.

The Pitchman raised the bejeweled object from the case, extended his hand from above the table to his left, and then released it.

Melvin was flummoxed when he saw that the doorknob didn't fall. Instead, it hovered there above the floor, in the space beside his center table at the height of The Pitchman's hip.

Melvin nearly toppled his chair when he saw something – some things – emerging from the knob.

It was like nature had exploded in his little ratty den. From the top of the doorknob sprang tree branches, crimson and leafless, knotted and gnarled. Dozens of them growing, stretching, as if reaching for the roof but stopping partway there.

From the bottom of the doorknob grew roots, thinner braided red tendrils that fell from it, descending to the ground until the knob was no longer floating but part of a larger standing mass.

For a moment, Melvin was looking at a tree the colour of blood, naked, twisted, and ancient. A moment later, the tree was turning into something else. The branches and roots expanded, thickened, filled out until they began to touch, eliminating the spaces between them. They smoothened out as Melvin rubbed eyes that his brain disbelieved, his mind having trouble accepting what he was seeing. He couldn't understand how there was now a scarlet-coloured door standing in the middle of his basement.

As this was happening, as the ornate floating doorknob finished turning to a tree and then a door, the walls – no longer only wavering or wobbling – began to shake, the entire room began to quake. Lucy was meowing wildly, his mother was screaming from upstairs,

"A rat! A rat!"

Melvin was shaking in his seat along with everything else around him, wondering what was going on, trying to pinpoint the exact moment he had lost his mind.

The Blood Red Door was the only steady thing in the trembling basement. It opened for The Pitchman without him having to reach out and twist the knob. From behind the incomprehensible door poured a thick mist, like smoke, the same unique hue of blue as The Pitchman's eyes.

The Pitchman stepped toward the door, was about to walk into the Blue Abyss on the other side of it. But, before he did so, he turned.

There was yowling from Lucy, screaming from his mother upstairs, and the sound of things shaking all over the room, yet Melvin heard The Pitchman clearly.

"Take heart, Mr. Cockburn! Take heart!"

Then he walked through the door. When it shut behind him, so too did Melvin's eyes. And all was dark and silent.

8

"Melvin! Damn it, boy! Get your skinny ass up here! Ain't you hear me screaming?"

Melvin jolted awake in his recliner. He looked around frantically. For some reason he expected to be in the middle of an earthquake. He was panicked, felt lost. His heart was racing, his mind was muddled.

"Must have been a dream," Melvin muttered, feeling unsettled but not knowing why. He looked over to the floor beside him, at his cat carrier. His cat was still inside of it despite the door being open. He wished that Lucy's decay were a dream too, rather than the waking nightmare that it was.

"You okay, little girl?" he whispered to her, snapping his fingers, trying to coax her out of the carrier. She ignored him, laying there limply, looking like death.

"Melvin!"

"I hear you, mom! I'm coming!" he screamed back before uttering a string of profanities aimed at his mother under his breath. Woozily, he stood up on unsteady legs, nearly fell back onto his seat. It was then he realized he didn't remember coming downstairs. Didn't remember putting the carrier down and opening the basement door. His last memory was of entering the house and having a shouting match with his mother. Then he had woken to the sound of her continuing to shout at him just now.

Worried that the stress of what was happening to Lucy was finally getting to him, Melvin took a deep breath, steadied himself, and made his way up the stairs as fast as his shaky legs could take him.

9

"What is it, mom? What's with all the noise?" Melvin asked in a huff, struggling to catch his breath following his run up the stairs and into the kitchen. His mother stood there with the small of her back pressed against the stove, her hands clasped together atop a sagging bosom he could see far too distinctly through one of the muumuus she wore around the house when she wasn't draped in a robe. She was shaking, clearly terrified.

It was a reversal of roles for them. Melvin had spent many miserable moments in this place, shaking and terrified. This part of the house was supposed to be a source of nourishment, a place for growth, for the enjoyment of simple things like hot pancakes, cold cereal, warm milk. Instead, it had been a place of mental torture for the young Melvin. This was where his mother had said to him many mean and hurtful things.

He couldn't help but think of those things whenever he was here interacting with the wretched woman who had birthed him. He was certain that if his mother ever did die, and if ghosts were real, that this was where hers would end up. The kitchen was where the bad energy was. To Melvin, it was a place where evil things like the soul of Moira Cockburn ought to linger.

"Should have had an abortion."

Melvin remembered those words every time he was in the kitchen with her. Those were words she would utter to him (or mutter to herself with him right beside her) on occasion. Such as the occasion she had been called to his school after Melvin had once again been beaten up by one of his classmates in the third grade. To Moira, it was clear even then that the boy was born to be a loser, something she had repeatedly told him starting not long after that day.

When he had entered the ninth grade and found out what having an abortion meant, he had immediately confronted her about why she would have said such a thing. He had also worked up the nerve to finally ask her where his father was. It was the first and only time he'd broached the topic since he had first inquired as a curious kindergartner.

On that day, upon hearing the four-year-old Melvin ask why other kids had daddies but not him, Moira's face had twisted into an illustration of rage. He would forever remember that unhinged expression. It was as though she had never expected the question from a son who lived alone with his mother. It was as though she had been offended by the innocent query. Felt personally attacked by it. Felt like she had to retaliate due to this perceived provocation.

Pressing that rage-twisted face into his, she had screamed, "Ain't I been daddy enough for you?" before she pulled back and slapped him twice about the cheek and ear, leaving him hearing a ringing sound for hours after. Then, she had told him never to ask about his dad again. Told him that she was both mom and dad and the only parent he needed. Informed him, spitting, seething, that he should count his blessings for having a mom and dad as good as her.

Melvin had believed that literally. For years after she had slapped him nearly silly as a four-year-old, his mother would inform him that she was both his parents, to the point that he thought she had undergone some process of self-fertilization. Believed that she had made him asexually.

Years later, in the ninth grade, when he had learned about the birds and the bees and how an unborn baby could be removed from a woman with a vacuum or a pair of forceps, he had felt he'd had no choice but to ask his mother why she might have wanted that for the embryonic version of him.

During this monumental confrontation, Melvin's mother had been sitting at the kitchen table, her favourite spot in the house. The area she frequented most. She had been reading one of her romance novels at the time, a bottle of wine in front of her, and a rapidly emptying glass of wine beside it.

She had beamed a rare smile at the then fourteen-year-old Melvin, who had been standing nervously across the table from where she had sat. Where she always sat. He could see the wine had stained her teeth purple, dyed her tongue that colour as well. He remembered that distinctly whenever he thought of the day his mother told him the story of his birth; that dark purple tongue and the poison it produced.

The story of Melvin's birth started with the fact that she had wanted to abort him, something that was illegal at the time of his conception. She had told her father this; she usually would have gone to her mother, but her mother had died of ovarian cancer the year prior.

Moira Cockburn had found herself in a situation she would never have imagined: her life falling apart as she, a woman of nearly forty years, cried to her newly widowed father. Telling him that she had accidentally gotten pregnant by someone she barely knew, letting him know that she was considering getting rid of the child.

Her purple tongue had wagged as she had poured more wine into her glass while telling the young Melvin that she should never have gone to her dad for comfort. She had hoped he would be supportive, the way her mother surely would have been, but her dad, Melvin Cockburn the first, had surprised her.

Her father, who had dived deep into his religion to deal with the loss of his wife, had let her know that he would disown her, and that Moira would burn in Hell, if she intentionally rid herself of the would-be child.

She had just lost her mother, she didn't want to lose her father as well. And she certainly didn't want to burn in Hell. Still, she had pleaded with her father, telling him that the man who had impregnated her was a stranger, and not exactly a good guy. Though she left out the details in telling her father what she would eventually tell her son.

Details such as her impregnator being married based on the band that had constricted his left ring finger. The ring she had felt against her flesh as he had fondled her while fucking her from behind. She also hadn't mentioned to her father that the man who had knocked her up was a police officer nearly twenty years her junior. Moira had told the young Melvin but not her dad that the cop had seduced her after pulling her over for speeding, and letting her know he didn't have to give her a ticket if he could buy her a drink instead. She didn't speak to her father of the seedy bar on the outskirts of town, the bathroom stall, being bent over the toilet during that one-night stand.

Her father, still relatively young, a man in his early sixties at the time, had said he would help to raise the child. It was either that or he would be out of her life completely. She had accepted his ultimatum. Agreed to keep her future bastard.

When she went into labour, her father was the first person she had called. He promised her he would meet her at the hospital right away. And wound up crushed beneath the wheels of a tractor-trailer in his haste to keep his word.

Moira Cockburn had found out her father was dead only minutes after giving birth to her son alone in the hospital and naming the boy after the man who had coerced her into having him. It was the circle of life, and it had tightened around her neck, strangling her.

Moira Cockburn and Melvin Cockburn II were both fatherless. And she had hated the police, her dead dad, and her son ever since then.

"Ain't you got ears, goddamnit? I said there's a *rat* running around up here!" She removed one of her loose skinned arms from her chest long enough to point to the corner of the kitchen. To point at the base of the small pantry cabinet.

He heard it before he saw it. A little creature crying, squeaking, nearly screaming, a shrill, discontenting sound. When he saw it, he understood why it sounded as it did. The mouse had run into one of the traps they had laid throughout the house. This one was located in the shallow recess at the bottom of the pantry.

His mother had seen (or thought she had seen) a mouse nearly fifteen years ago and had been paranoid about them ever since. At her urging, the two had laid at least a dozen traps throughout the house. Snap traps, sticky traps; she even had a couple of those high tech ultrasonic rodent repellent devices plugged into their walls.

Despite the prevalence of traps throughout the house, this was the first mouse he had encountered since his mother's claim of seeing one over a decade prior. If there had been a rodent back then, he liked to think that Lucy had prevented them from seeing any more. But now that she was incapacitated, perhaps the little critters had become emboldened.

"Well? What are you waiting for? Will you get that fucking rat out of my house?"

"It's not a rat," he said impatiently, impetuously, splitting hairs when the distinction made no difference. It was a loose rodent either way, and his mother wanted it out.

But it wasn't just any mouse. To Melvin it seemed familiar even while it looked out of place. It not only looked out of place because it was stuck there, writhing, twitching, its upper half moving while its lower portion remained lax and limp, the bar of the trap having snapped its spine in two, but because it wasn't the usual brown, grey, or black mouse one might picture scurrying around a lower middle class home like theirs. It was a stark white rodent. Like something that might be found in a lab. Or in a pet store. Not to be made a pet but to be made into pet food.

He was struck with a feeling of immense déjà vu as he looked upon the little creature.

"I don't care what it is! Get it *out!*"

How lungs that old could still make such noise, Melvin would never know. But this last scream was shrill enough to make him jump where he stood before immediately walking toward the broken mouse in the trap.

He took a deep breath as he approached it, feeling his heart beating faster, his nerves raw. He was scared, he realized. Scared of a tiny mouse that had been broken nearly in half in its pursuit of an ancient smear of peanut butter. Scared it might bite him, that it might infect him. Melvin was scared to touch the thing at all. He exhaled with effort, reached for the mouse's tail, and nearly leapt back when the thing turned its head toward him and squealed, its black eyes wide and watery.

Did it know it was broken? Melvin wondered. Was it hoping he would put it out of its misery? Or maybe it believed that he could save it.

He thought twice about touching its tail. He grabbed the base of the trap instead, behind the mouse, where it couldn't reach back and bite him, where its malfunctioning legs were incapable of kicking out and scratching him the way its front paws threatened to do.

Melvin proceeded to leave the kitchen, the sound of his mother sighing in relief followed him around the corner as he made his way to the front door.

When he got there, he had a thought. A thought that felt like a memory. Words that weren't his own:

In order for your cat to live, you have to feed her life.

There was that unsettling feeling of déjà vu again.

He looked back to see if his mother was watching him from the kitchen. She wasn't. Apparently, she trusted him enough to do this task without her constant badgering.

He opened the door and counted down from ten, still watching the hallway, the entry to the kitchen. At the end of his countdown, he closed the door.

"You won't have to worry about that mouse anymore, mom!" he shouted into the house, the mouse in question still in his hand.

He heard no response. No 'thank you,' no appreciation. What else was new? But he didn't care. Because he had something he had to do. Something important. One last attempt at saving his cat.

"You didn't get all broken for no reason, little guy," he whispered to the mouse as he walked through the hallway. "Your sacrifice will be for the greater good..." he said, attempting to embrace optimism for one of the few times in his life.

Melvin headed to the basement, his head full of doubts, his heart full of hope.

10

Lucy looked at her owner skeptically as Melvin knelt in front of the cat carrier she still refused to exit.

He had carefully and painstakingly removed the mouse from the trap, his stomach roiling as the thing screamed its high-pitch scream. He had nearly thrown up as he'd pried the bar from the little creature's broken back and seen the shift of the bifurcated spine. The bones rose and pressed against the skin, visible under the creature's fur in places they should not have been. The front legs pawed furiously at Melvin, then at the air, as he carried it by the tail. The back legs hung limply, flopping to the mouse's sides.

He now dangled the little white mouse in front of the carrier, feeling silly for not just throwing it outside for nature to take care of it like his mother had wanted. Feeling like he had been a desperate fool for thinking this might work.

But, as she always did (at least before she had become sick), his cat found a way to cheer him up. She did so with a single sound, a high-pitched meow. Her indication that she was hungry.

"Yeah, Lucy? You hungry?"

She meowed again, and he allowed himself to believe that she might be open to eating something for the first time in days. When she crawled slowly out of the carrier, he felt further encouraged.

The mouse squeaked loudly, repeatedly. It seemed to understand that it was going to be a meal. He dropped it in front of his cat. It tried to run away but couldn't move its back legs. The result was a desperate, frenzied upper body crawl that made Melvin feel sorrow for the tiny creature.

"It'll be over soon, little mouse," he said. And he was right.

Lucy swiped at the mouse, batted it, playing with her food. But not for long. Grabbing the mouse by its flaccid tail, she dragged it toward her. Melvin watched, his hands clutched together at his thighs, his heart beating as though he was waiting for the last lotto number of a potentially winning ticket to be called.

Lucy looked up at him, and he clearly understood the expression on her face. *Is this for me? Am I allowed to have it?*

"Go on, girl. You need its life."

And, as if understanding her owner, Lucy moved with an energy he didn't think she still possessed. In two swift moves the mouse became dinner. She turned the rodent onto its back, then brought her face down to its exposed underbelly. Then there was blood. More of it than he thought could have come out of such a small thing.

Squeaking, squeaking, then silence from the mouse. And famished growling from his little cat as she dined on an animal for the first time in her life. A life he hoped this once moving meal could extend.

Then it was over. The rodent stopped squirming; the white fur around Lucy's mouth was red. There was blood surrounding what had once been the mouse. It was now a red and pink thing with its innards either missing or spilled, a small bag of skin and bones.

As much as he was glad to see her finally eating, the sight of it all revolted Melvin. He fought the urge to throw up, having to use all his strength to keep himself from fleeing to his laundry sink and emptying his stomach into it.

It was his love for his cat that kept him there watching her, her face red, her body still weak, all of her gaunt, far too thin.

As if sensing his observance of her while licking at the blood on the floor, Lucy looked up at him. A drop of crimson liquid dangled from a whisker. She made a sound almost as sad as the mouse's final squeaking; a mewling noise which Melvin understood perfectly.

Life, is what that sound meant, what that look meant, too. It was a request, an urging.

More life.

And that was what he planned to give her.

11

The improvement Melvin saw in Lucy was nearly instantaneous. She didn't retreat into her carrier as he expected her to. Instead, after devouring the mouse, she walked – still slowly, still struggling – over to the recliner and waited patiently for him to sit so she could sit with him. She would have jumped up and waited on the arm of the recliner once upon a time, but she currently didn't have that kind of energy.

But you will soon, Melvin thought eagerly. Though it didn't take long for that eagerness to turn into unease as he looked at the remnants of the rodent on the ground. It was impossible to tell it had once been white. Now it was a collection of bloodied bits and pieces, smears and stains on the concrete floor. The sight was enough for his stomach to finally protest against what his eyes had fed it.

He ran through the curtain which parted his living area from the laundry room and made his way to the sink. Threw up in it. Afterward, he turned on the water without looking down at what had come out of him, fearing that the sight of it would make him sick again. Wiping his mouth with the back of his hand, then wiping the back of his hand on his pants, Melvin wondered if he would be back here at the sink in a few moments, throwing up again. The mouse wouldn't be the last revolting thing he would see this evening.

It was time to change Lucy's coverings. It was time to face her tumour.

Since the lump had grown out of control, he'd had to dress it. Had to dress her. He would have to remove her onesie, then the pair of maxi pads acting like a diaper to soak up the discharge that spilled endlessly out of her. He had to change these three times a day to avoid the tumour becoming infected, to avoid the skin around it becoming further full of rashes and abrasions. It was torture every time. For him, for her. They both hated the process.

Leaning against the sink, looking at the curtain parting the laundry room from the living room and dreading what was on the other side, Melvin took a deep breath and went to face the thing that was slowly killing his cat.

12

"Ouch!" Melvin said after Lucy scratched him. He looked down at his hand. Only one of her claws had penetrated his skin. The flesh revealed by the cut was momentarily white before it became red, blood welling from the sliver of a wound and eventually beading down the back of his hand.

He was delighted to see this.

As he looked at the cut, his free hand holding Lucy down on the couch, she swiped at him again. But this time he avoided it. She was much slower these days.

"Bad cat," he said to Lucy. The words were insincere, they emerged from him upon a chuckle. While he wasn't glad to have been scratched, he was glad that Lucy had the strength again to do the scratching.

He currently had her pinned, as gently as he could, to the couch by her shoulders. She was laying on her side. He was preparing to swap her Toronto Maple Leafs onesie for her Toronto Blue Jays onesie, a fresh pair of maxi pads attached to it.

Two months ago, when this process had become necessary, he had made the mistake of thinking he could remove the onesie and change the pads within it while giving Lucy's body and tumour a chance to breathe. He'd quickly understood his mistake when, once he had released Lucy, she had turned her head into herself and begun to attack the open abscess on her midsection. Licking and suckling at the tumour, chewing at the foul smelling, fluid-filled opening in the middle of the baseball sized pustule. She had done this while making the noise of a rabid ravenous animal, a hunger-maddened creature allowed to finally gnaw on a piece of meaty bone after days of being starved.

By the time he had grabbed her and pulled her head from the middle of her body, she had chewed her tumour bloody. Thick red and pale yellow gelatin-like strings had been hanging from her face.

And that hadn't been the only mistake he had made while originally adjusting to the process of dressing Lucy's ailment. When he had first attempted to put the onesie on her, she had clawed and bit at him ceaselessly; growled, hissed, yowled, made near-demonic noises. She had left him gouged and bloodied that first time. Melvin had made sure to wear his mother's gardening gloves, along with a thick sweater, each time he changed her thereafter. That was until she had become too weak to put up much of a struggle.

For the last few days, she had simply lain there, growling but unable to fight against this process she abhorred so strongly. It had been heartbreaking to see.

Now she was fighting again, and despite a bit of his blood having been shed, Melvin was thrilled. He was also thrilled to see her tumour once he finally removed the soiled onesie from her, which was something he never would have expected. The tumour, for the first time since it had appeared, seemed to be getting better and not worse. Though 'better,' in this case, was still a horrendous sight. It was a large, naked, open boil. It reminded him of a volcano made of pink-red flesh, its center full of green-yellow lava, always looking as though it were ready to erupt. But, unless Melvin's eyes were deceiving him, the pus-filled hole in the center was smaller than it had been the day before. It looked as though it might be in the early stages of closing.

It had started as a little lump beneath Lucy's fur only four months ago. It never seemed to bother her, even when he touched it. He had convinced himself it was something benign until it had begun to worsen. It had grown, the fur falling away, the colour going from pink to red. It was at that point he had taken her to the vet.

It had cost him hundreds of dollars for the tests that would simply determine if Lucy had a terminal illness. Melvin had paid that fee using money from the miniscule monthly financial assistance he received from the government on account of his learning disability (or, as his mother would say, on account of his general retardation).

When the bad news from the biopsy had come back, he had been asked to pay much more for a procedure, a removal of the mass that couldn't guarantee the cancer would be entirely cut out, or that the tumour wouldn't return.

He didn't have nearly enough money to afford what the veterinarian had said was his only chance to save Lucy. In a state of desperation, he had turned to a person he tried his best never to turn to. Unfortunately for the severely introverted, incredibly friendless, resourceless, and connectionless Melvin, this was the only person he *could* turn to.

On his knees in the kitchen, the place he hated most, Melvin had begged his mother to help him. To help Lucy. Moira, as usual, had been dressed in one of her garish robes, sitting at the table with a romance novel.

Wine glass. Wine bottle.

Purple teeth.

One would have assumed he had learned by then not to approach her in that state. Moira Cockburn was a mean person. She was an even meaner drunk.

"Maybe if you weren't such a retard, you'd have a job by now. You'd be able to support yourself," she had said, slurring as she sprayed purple-red spittle across the white dining table. And when Melvin had fallen from his knees to his ass, as though the words had physically struck him, as though they had been punctuated with boots and knuckles, she had continued by saying, "Stop snivelling like a little sissy." She had paused to slurp from her wine glass. "My God, Melly, when are you gonna be a man? Cats die. People die. Things die. You have to be strong enough to cope."

He had wondered why she wasn't one of those things already dead as her purple tongue wagged while a cruel smile stretched across her face. Melvin, in that moment, had believed she would live forever, and would torment him for that same measure of time.

That was how Moira had declined his plea for the money to save his cat. By calling him a retard (oh how he hated that word!), by telling him he wasn't a man. By insisting he accept things as they were. Suck it up. Cope. Melvin had watched Lucy slowly dying ever since.

But now, thanks to the life she had received from the mouse, she was fighting again. Clawing and growling, hissing and biting at him as he removed and replaced her coverings. Melvin was as happy as he had been in months

Once she was dressed, she settled down. She stopped attempting to gnaw at her tumour and at his hand, allowing him to carry her from the couch without much fuss. Placing her on his lap as he sat on the recliner, he turned on the television and changed the station to NBC just in time to watch a new episode of *Seinfeld*, his favourite sitcom. For the first time in a long while, he was able to relax.

Lucy purring contentedly on his lap, something funny on the screen, Melvin stroked his cat and smiled, wishing, hoping it could be like this from now on.

13

Lucy was worse again the next day.

Melvin woke up to an empty lap and a sinking feeling in his stomach. He lurched in his seat, looked for Lucy, certain for some reason that she would be gone. He didn't see her anywhere at first. Then he looked closely through the slits of her carrier, saw her yellow-orange fur, and breathed a sigh of relief.

For a moment he thought it might have been a dream; the mouse, Lucy feeling better, them enjoying a fun night of cuddles and television as they had for so many years prior to this supposedly terminal illness. But it couldn't have been a dream, there was evidence to say otherwise in the form of a mouse splayed open on the floor. Its blood had coagulated, hardening into a brown-red paste around it.

"You okay, little Lucy?" he cooed.

He received no response.

After trying and failing to lure her out, he was able to pull Lucy from the carrier. It was time to change her again. He put on his gloves and a sweater to do so, but, unlike yesterday, Lucy put up no fight. She was prone and listless once more.

That was dismaying enough for Melvin. What made it worse was that the tumour had reverted back to its fully festering state. The positive effects of consuming the mouse were apparently short lived.

More life.

He remembered the look on Lucy's face when she had indicated that request. And now it was time for him to give her what she wanted. What she needed.

Without wasting any more time, he threw on a jacket, grabbed his keys and wallet, put Lucy back inside of her carrier, and headed to the only place he knew that could provide his cat with the life she needed.

14

Melvin received strange looks as soon as he stepped into the pet store at Saturn City Center, the mall in the heart of the city. By then, he had come to expect them.

He had been receiving strange looks since he'd walked into the shopping center. He had been on the receiving end of sideways stares and askance glances when he'd been on the bus headed there as well. By the time he got to PJ's Pets on the lower level of the mall, he understood that leaving home in his Toronto Argonauts hooded sweatshirt and pajama pants hadn't been a wise idea in terms of not attracting derisive attention. Walking around with a cat carrier didn't seem normal either.

Despite feeling extremely self-conscious and slightly embarrassed, Melvin pushed on for the sake of Lucy. He went to the reptile section of the pet shop and spoke to the employee there. She was a tall white woman in her late teens or early twenties. She had a brown ponytail and piercings in her ears, her nose, her lip. He imagined there were other places pierced on her body that he could never hope to see. Melvin asked her for the mice that one might buy to feed a snake.

"No problem, sir. Live or frozen?"

"Life… I mean, live. She needs them alive."

"That's how mine is, too," the employee said with a smile, a welcome change of expression from the bewildered look she had given him when he had strolled into the reptile section with a cat. "What kind of snake do you have?"

"No snake," Melvin said, regretting the sentence he was speaking even as he spoke it. "They're for her." He nodded to his carrier. To Lucy.

And there was that bewildered look again.

"Ummmm... You want to buy live mice for your cat?"

Melvin shrugged. Said,

"It's the only thing she'll eat."

The pet store employee had gone to get the live mice without asking any further questions, likely wanting him to get out of the store without complicating her shift. Melvin was glad for that. He didn't understand what was happening with Lucy let alone know how to explain it.

After leaving the pet store with nearly a dozen mice, and proceeding to his next stop – the Shoppers Drug Mart which was also on the lower level of the mall – he felt he had to explain his next unusual purchase to the cashier at the drugstore.

The young Black teenager with closely shorn hair looked from his cat carrier to the small cage containing ten mice, then to the item he had placed on her counter. And, though they shared no similar features, the bewilderment on her face was identical to that on the girl's in the pet store.

"They're not for me, they're for her," he said, an echo of his previous statement to the pet store employee. It was not any more helpful this time than it had been during that encounter.

She looked from him to the package of *U by Kotex* menstrual pads in front of her. She scanned them. Red digits showed up on the display above the register.

"That'll be two ninety-nine," the cashier informed him, reading aloud what he had already seen on the display. Her eyes refused to meet his even as she held her hand out for his money.

After he had paid, Melvin thought he heard her whispering loudly to the cashier across the lane from her as he headed out of the store. They were likely judging his outfit and everything he carried, making fun of him, laughing together in that nearly telepathic way that only shitty teenagers could when they ridiculed someone while still in sight of them. He shrugged it off. It didn't matter. The only thing that did matter was making Lucy better.

After leaving the pharmacy, and while heading for one of the mall's many exits, it was more of the same: odd looks, peculiar stares, naked bafflement.

Melvin noticed the looks. Paid no mind. Didn't care.

Carrying his cat, her mice, and a bag of menstrual pads, Melvin giggled, his renewed hope bursting out of him involuntarily. It was not a loud laugh, just a bit of a titter. But it was loud enough to catch the attention of those who weren't already looking at him.

He picked up the pace. He did so not to avoid the looks, not out of embarrassment, but because he couldn't wait to get back home and begin the process of saving his cat's life, one rodent at a time.

15

Melvin had been surprised when Lucy ate two of the mice, one immediately after the other. Her appetite was voracious, perhaps having been worked up by being in close proximity to her inevitable food on the bus ride back home. A bus ride that had involved the same stares and looks of revulsion he had experienced in the mall.

A few people moved away from him when he had sat down in the bus, scuttling further back into the public transit vehicle, staring, sneering, and whispering all the while. He couldn't understand it. But it didn't matter. The rest of the world and their judgment be damned, his cat was going to have all the life she needed.

It had been the same as the first time; Lucy opened up the mice's middles, ate the contents of their insides, left the rest on the floor.

Instantaneously, she had been improved.

After the second mouse, she had purred serenely, going from laying nearly motionless to walking around the confines of the basement, sniffing around the area, then pawing at the curtains between the living room and the laundry room before hesitantly working her way through them. It was as if she was discovering the area for the first time. Her curiosity was back, and Melvin was overjoyed.

But the improvement to her condition didn't last. Not for as long as Melvin had expected, and not for long at all. He had believed that each mouse would improve her health incrementally. He had hoped that eating all of them would get her to the point of full recovery. However, after three days and ten dead and devoured mice, Lucy was right back to where she had been when he had last brought her home from the vet.

Thin, tumour at full fester, lethargic. Dying.

"We'll figure it out, Lucy," he assured her, though he didn't completely believe his own words. Melvin sat down on the floor next to Lucy, petting her tenderly as she lay on the old towel next to his recliner. The frayed rag had become her bed since she had fallen ill.

The last mouse had been eaten the previous evening, and Melvin was chagrined to see that its positive effects had dissipated at some point in the night.

"More life," Melvin whispered to himself as he sat cross-legged beside his cat. He was contemplating those words, understanding now that perhaps it couldn't just be more mice; his solution wasn't just more life but *bigger* life. Lucy needed something other than a measly mouse or two.

He wondered if he should buy a rabbit from the pet store, or locate a farm that might sell him some live chickens. Another thought that crossed his mind was trapping a racoon. But trying to feed the innards of a live racoon to his cat seemed like a losing proposition.

He settled on the idea of getting two rabbits for the time being. Once he saw how effective they might be, he would re-evaluate the situation. He wasn't confident at all, he was worried the result would be the same.

Just as Melvin was beginning to feel truly hopeless again for the first time in days, the last person he had ever believed might help him find a solution did exactly that.

"Melvin! Melvin, get up here! That damn dog is in the yard again!" Melvin's mother cried from upstairs. The sound of her startled him badly, so deep in thought had he been.

'That damn dog' was Obi, the Jack Russell Terrier of one Mrs. Chloe Anita Thames, who lived three doors down from Melvin and his mother. She was Melvin's favourite neighbour. The only neighbour who spoke to him or acknowledged his existence in a way that didn't reek of mockery.

Obi was an unruly dog. He had the habit of getting out of his back yard and running into the yards of the other residents on the street. When Obi got out, anyone who found him knew to bring him back to Mrs. Thames. Despite being a bit of a nuisance and a masterful escape artist, he was a good dog, or at least a friendly one, and no one in the neighbourhood minded his escapades. No one except for Melvin's mother.

"You hear me, boy! Come get this dog, or I'm calling the pound!"

"No, mom!" he cried out to her. Then, lower, to himself, "Fuck. Why's she gotta be such a cunt about everything?"

His initial concern was for both the dog and its owner. It wouldn't be the first time his mother had reported the sprightly terrier to the authorities. If it happened again, Obi would be taken for good; rehomed or put to sleep. That was the last thing his owner needed.

Mrs. Thames was a sweet lady, severely down on her luck as it was. And her dog wasn't causing anyone any harm. But his mother couldn't stand anything being happy and free.

"Well then you better haul ass and get this thing! I got the phone in my hand!"

"Do *not* call the pound!" He rose from beside his cat on the floor. As he did so, Lucy looked up at him intently. She made that particular meowing sound again. The one that he understood as though it were a word from the English language. The one that indicated hunger.

More life, she reminded him.

He looked down at her, contemplating what he knew he had to do before nodding in agreement. The mice were not enough, the rabbits might not be either, but this, what she was suggesting now, could be exactly what Lucy needed.

"Don't you call the pound, mom! I'll take care of the dog!"

Then he ran upstairs to do so.

16

When Melvin got upstairs, he saw that his mother had been telling the truth. She did have the phone in her hand. She had carried it from the cradle near the microwave to the back door. The usually coiled cord was stretched, straight and taut, as Moira Cockburn stood looking through the window of the door into her back yard.

From over her shoulder, Melvin saw little Obi in the yard, chasing his own tail before he made his way toward Moira's prized petunia plants which grew along the faded and peeling wood privacy fence separating the Cockburn's yard from their neighbour's.

"If that mutt gets into those flowers, so help me, they'll be gassing him at the pound by the morning!"

Obi sniffed at the petunias. Moira began to press the buttons on the phone.

Melvin couldn't have that. The dog needed to live.

In four long strides, he was across the kitchen. He snatched the phone from his mother's hands before she could complete dialing the number for animal services.

It was the most physical he had been with her since he had grabbed at a toy she had taken from him when he was five. She had spent the following half hour turning his ass red and welted with the handle of a feather duster in response. He hadn't attempted anything like that again until this moment. He never thought it was something he would ever do, never believed he was capable of such an aggressive act toward his mother. Which was why he looked down at the phone in his hand as though he was surprised to see it there, as though it had materialized in his palm all at once. He looked up at his mother to see that the shock he felt was mirrored on her face.

The two stood there by the back door, staring at each other. Her in disbelief, he defiantly. For Melvin, this was long overdue.

"I *said* I will take care of it," he told her through gritted teeth. His words ended their staring contest. A contest which he won. After breaking eye contact with her son, Moira turned back to the window. Melvin did the same. Both looked outside just in time to see that Obi had his leg raised over Moira's flowers.

Audibly fuming, a shrill whistling noise coming from her nose as she breathed, Moira looked from the yard momentarily to glare at Melvin before returning her attention to Obi.

"*You?* Take care of it?" she barked at him over her shoulder. "Since when have you ever been able to take care of any goddamn th–"

Her words were cut off abruptly when Melvin smashed the receiver of the phone into the back of her head. The blow was so hard, so severe, it moved the octogenarian several feet. She stumbled forward, stopping only when her face bounced off the window. Moira Cockburn let out a shocked yelp followed by a groan of pain.

Melvin was surprised yet again; this time because his mother wasn't unconscious. Her knees had buckled, but she hadn't left her feet. She was slumped against the door, using it for leverage as she tried to turn and face her son.

Tough old bitch.

"I'll take care of everything," he whispered. At this, she made a muddled sound, a noise with a question mark at the end of it. Some contorted version of "Huh?", "What?", or "Why?" Perhaps the small, inflected grunt meant all three.

She was dazed, confused, but somehow not falling.

Melvin marveled as his mother lurched and pushed herself from the door, becoming steadier on her feet with each movement. She twisted herself around, managed to face him.

On the window he saw a blotch of red fluid dripping down the glass. On Moira's face Melvin saw where that red on the window had come from. Blood gushed out of her nose, ran over her lips, dripped down her chin. In the middle of her forehead was a lump he could see growing by the millisecond. Yet she still had awareness in her eyes.

Awareness and hatred.

The same hatred he had recognized in those eyes since he was old enough to understand what hatred was, and to accept that a mother could feel such an emotion for their child.

She was going to speak again, perhaps more coherently, possibly to mock him for the millionth time in his life. For attacking her from behind. For not being man enough to be able to knock her out even with the benefit of an ambush. Even while wielding a weapon. He could see all of that in her eyes. And he could see that she was going to call him pathetic. Or worse.

But he wouldn't let her.

With all his might, he reared back. With the phone in his hand, he struck his mother across the jaw as she opened her mouth to speak. This time she crumpled instantly, bones and loose skin rattling and flapping to the floor. Moira landed on her knees, then fell on her side.

To Melvin's relief, those hateful, judging eyes were finally closed.

17

Melvin thought he had killed his mother at first. He heard the phone connect with her skull, heard the crack of hard plastic against jawbone and the jingle of the ringer as the cradle was ripped from the wall by his swinging of the receiver. The phone had fallen to the floor along with Moira Cockburn. And Melvin had been sure she was dead.

Killing her hadn't been his intention. He needed her alive.

More life.

He could hear Lucy meowing from downstairs, speaking of her hunger. He needed his mother's life for his cat.

Seeing Moira fall to the floor, he had worried that he'd let his anger get the best of him. That he had hit her too hard. But his tough, old, bitch of a mother had still been breathing, her midsection expanding and contracting slowly but steadily.

Good, he had thought, he too beginning to breathe again after having held his breath as he watched his mother fall. Then he had quickly raced to the basement to get two things: duct tape and his cat.

Now they were all together, the three of them, sitting at the kitchen table like they never had before. Like a little family should. Though not in a way that any normal family would.

On the table was a dying cat, laying there, waiting for her life to be extended. In one chair was that cat's owner, desperate to save her. And across from him, in another chair, naked and duct taped to it, was the person who was set to be the source of Lucy's salvation:

Melvin's mother, a human sacrifice to save his cat. Or so he hoped.

Her jaw was blue, her forehead swollen and purple. Much of the rest of her face was red. Her nose, which had bled badly, was now congested, clotted blood filled her nostrils. Dried and drying blood created an almost comical moustache and goatee over and around the piece of tape that covered her lips, keeping the sock he had stuffed inside her mouth secure.

But nothing was comical about this situation to Melvin. His cat just wasn't eating.

"C'mon Lucy. It's life, just like you asked for. *Eat*."

When she didn't respond, he picked the cat up. Melvin walked around the table with Lucy in his hands, carrying her in a way that made her back legs dangle and her front legs stick out straight ahead of her like a George A. Romero zombie. He set her down on his mother's pale, doughy, multi-coloured, vein-streaked thighs. He pushed Lucy forward until her nose and mouth were touching his mother's naked torso. Above her belly button, between her sagging breasts.

Melvin had taped his mother's legs to the legs of the seat she was on. Her hands were taped behind her back, behind the back of the chair. A reel of tape went around her shoulders, the tops of her breasts. More tape around the chair at the point of her hips, her lower belly, the bottom of her breasts. She could wriggle – which was what she was doing now, her shoulders shimmying as she squirmed, as she tried to shift in her seat – but she couldn't move. Not in any significant way. And if her restraints didn't stop her, Melvin would. For Moira Cockburn, there would be no escaping her son.

"*Eat!*" he repeated discontentedly to his cat, not understanding why she wouldn't. This was what she needed. This was what she had asked for. He continued to press her face against his mother. Nothing. Not even a nibble.

Melvin put Lucy down on the table. He paced the kitchen floor, looking periodically from the decades-old linoleum to his nearly century old mother. He couldn't make sense of the muffled sounds she was making on account of the sock in her mouth, the duct tape on her lips. But by the panicked look in her eyes – they bulged and darted back and forth between Melvin and Lucy on the table – he thought she was scared. He wondered if she was remorseful as well.

"You brought this on yourself, mom." He walked back over to the table, but not to his mother. Instead, he knelt on one knee until he was face to face with his cat. To Lucy, he said, "C'mon, Luce. *Please* just eat. More life, remember? *More life.* Here it is."

He was on the verge of breaking down. He felt his face growing hot, his eyes blurring, brimming with freshly formed tears that threatened to be shed. But he wasn't sad, he was angry. He whipped his head around. Stood and faced his mother.

"Maybe you're too nasty! Too old and bitter for her. Maybe you're more disgusting than those fucking mice you're always so scared of. She ate *them*. She had no problem eating *them!*"

He stepped to Moira gradually, moving an inch at a time, slowly getting closer. His fists were bundled bones by his sides, his eyes were slits in his head. And they were clear, his eyes; the tears which had threatened to fall had been burned away by red-hot rage.

His mother, in response, began to move her head back and forth as frantically as her eighty-year-old neck would allow. Her shoulders wriggled, her chair squeaked against the linoleum as she desperately tried to retreat. The muffled sounds she made grew louder as she fought to speak.

He considered the tape over her mouth.

Would she scream if he removed it? Would she cry for help?

Was that exactly what he wanted to hear?

It might make him feel better, after all these years, to hear her weakened. To hear her humbled in a way that time and age and the disesteem of most of those who knew her had not been able to do.

"Of course you have something to say," he growled. And then, overwhelmed by curiosity, *needing* to hear what that something might be, he reached for the tape over her mouth. He wanted to feel better about how this had all turned out. Wanted to be consoled somehow because his cat wouldn't eat his mother. He knew he would be soothed by the sounds of this monster who had birthed him begging. Pleading.

Then what would he do? After he heard what he wanted to hear, would there be any coming back from this?

The tape made a ripping noise as he pulled it from her wrinkled lips. The drying blood that had been coating both it and her lips came off with the tape. She spit the sock from her mouth. It landed softly on her lap. She gasped, inhaled unobstructed air after being forced to breathe through a blood clotted nose. Her face was white and blue, red and purple, pale and bruised, bloodied and agitated.

Melvin was horrified to see that on Moira's multicoloured face a smirk had appeared, a defiant little smile. Not an expression of regret. There was nothing on that face that indicated begging and pleading.

"I knew I gave birth to a retard, but I didn't know you were batshit crazy. Your goddamn cat ain't gonna eat me, 'cause your goddamn cat–"

He grabbed the sock from her naked lap as she was speaking, slammed it back into her mouth. He then slapped the tape across her face so violently it caused her nose to bleed again. He left his hand there, over her mouth and nose, feeling her warm blood pooling against his palm. This is how he would end it. He would smother

her. She would drown in a handful of her own blood. But then came a sound. From beside him, from the table.

Little Lucy meowing.

Lucy saying *Feed me.*

"I've tried to feed you, Lucy. You won't eat your food. The mice don't work anymore, and you won't eat..." he looked down at his mother, whose eyes were wide, the whites no longer white. They were yellow, lined with red veins surrounding green irises which showed only black hatred. No regret. No sorrow. They mocked him even as she fought for air against his hand. "...You won't eat *this*..." Melvin continued. "I just don't know what to do!"

Grief wracked his body then. Those tears that had threatened and then evaporated were back, and this time they fell. As did he, to his knees in front of his bound and naked mother.

He was now level with his cat, who continued to voice her hunger, her desperate cries adding to his dismay and frustration. Just when that frustration was going to culminate in a scream, he heard a voice inside of his head. A familiar voice that wasn't his own. Perhaps a voice from a dream, maybe someone he had heard on television. It was a thin and tinny tone.

Take heart, Mr. Cockburn... Take heart!

His head snapped up. He looked at his mother. At her chest. Then looked at Lucy.

As if knowing what he was thinking, glad that he was finally understanding, she turned her meowing into one long, low, excited yowl. The sound she made was one of encouragement, a sound that let him know he had been going about things the entirely wrong way but he was now on the right track.

He got up from his knees. Left the kitchen table for the kitchen counter. Walked toward the block of knives.

From it he removed an eight inch chef's knife. It was the sharpest of his mother's collection, but it could stand to be sharper for what he had in mind. Following the knife, he withdrew the honing steel, the instrument meant to sharpen.

Melvin slashed the knife against the steel. Relished the sound of metal on metal. The sound of something deadly being made deadlier.

"Of course," he said to himself, around the sound of steel on steel in his hands. "Lucy doesn't have to eat her alive, she only has to eat what *keeps* her alive."

In his head there was a chant. It was in that same familiar but foreign voice. And it was saying two words, repeating them:

Take heart! Take heart!

From his cat, that approving yowl.

Still sharpening the knife, Melvin made his way back to his mother and brought the tip of the blade to her chest. There was no mocking in her eyes now. He was sure she wouldn't be smirking if he could see her mouth. Her head rocked back and forth, her body shook. Again, he wanted to hear what she might have to say, but this time he kept the sock in, the tape on.

There would be too much screaming.

18

It would have been easy to kill Moira. To plunge the knife in, take it out. Thrust it in again, then again, perhaps adding a twist or two of the handle during the process. But murder wasn't his intent, at least not immediately. What Melvin required was his mother's heart, still beating, to serve to his starving cat.

It was the life she needed.

The tip of the knife went into his mother's chest like any sharp knife through any soft thing. He started in the center of her body, at her sternum. Then he began to cut his way down. Blood first followed the blade, then overwhelmed it, a flowing fall around his knife and down her belly.

Too much blood. It was obscuring his goal, making an already difficult process more so. Melvin's goal was to sacrifice his mother to his cat. To take her heart and feed it to this creature that had reached a godly level of reverence in his mind. Like the Aztecs to their Sun God. Melvin could never remember the name of that God, and the forgetting of it bothered him slightly. But he recalled enough of the history; he remembered watching and rewatching a video on the subject of the ancient Aztecs and their sacrifices during his lonely days in high school. That was back when he had first realized that television and videos would be his only friends from then on out. Unliked, unpopular, practically unable to read, Melvin's TV and VCR were his only method of escaping. Of travelling to places that were not the place he was.

One of those places had been ancient Mexico, before it had been conquered and colonized by the Spanish. Through his television, Melvin had been transported to the Aztec pyramids, where their priests had lain slaves, citizens, women, children, infants, and prisoners of war down on stone slabs at the top of these towering sacred temples. These holy men had opened up their victims' chests with razor-sharp obsidian blades, extracted their still-beating hearts, sent their bodies rolling down the temple stairs.

The Aztecs performed this bloody and barbaric ritual dozens of times daily, and tens of thousands of times each year. All for the sake of appeasing a deity they had never seen. A deity the Aztec priests believed needed human sacrifices to keep the sun moving across the sky, to prevent the world from ending in darkness. One who required those priests to feast on the freshly removed hearts, and to wear the skin of the person whose life they had given to their God. A deity who did not exist. But Melvin's deity existed. And she was right there with him.

Little Lucy, cat Goddess. And she was eager for his sacrifice.

She was yowling her approval at him as he continued to cut. Encouraging him, reminding him of her hunger. Of her need to heal.

He removed his shirt and used it as a towel, pressing it against the wide-open wound that was his mother's midsection. Blotting and absorbing the blood, he disregarded the little whimpers that were stuck in Moira Cockburn's throat.

"It didn't have to be you, mom. It didn't. But you just... You just never *quit...*"

On his knees, he backed up and took a look at the wound from a greater distance, like an artist taking note of the paint they had brushed upon a canvas. With the cut, he was content. Through the severed skin, the parted flesh, he saw what the challenge would be: a plate of bone covering the heart he and his cat needed, viscera showing in the gap below it.

Moira was unconscious now. Every few seconds, he would check her pulse to ensure she was alive. Each time he felt it there, unsteady as it was, he thought the same thing: *Tough old bitch.*

But she was losing too much blood, her pulse becoming fainter. He had to hurry if he wanted to remove her beating heart.

Trying to keep his stomach from emptying, he ignored the revulsion arising from what he had done, and what he had to do next.

Abandoning the knife on the already bloody floor, Melvin took a deep breath, then, knowing that he didn't have the time or resources to break open the chest bone, he went up and in from beneath it.

He plunged his hand into the open wound he had created in his mother, shoved it under her ribcage, pushed until his forearm was surrounded by the meat of her; by organs, blood, and tissue.

He felt wetness, he felt warmth. Most importantly, he felt a vibration, a weak thumping inside of his mother's body. He followed that pulsing sensation while struggling to stave off panic.

Time. He was running out of time.

Steadying himself as much as he could, Melvin reached further into his mother, his forearm pressing and pushing away her innards, his wrist rubbing against ribcage. He was almost there, was within inches of that pulsating place in her chest. But then he felt a blockage. Something separating the stomach from the chest. Something stopping him from getting to his goal. An obstruction he needed to cut his way past.

As Melvin considered reaching for the knife on the floor, Moira Cockburn regained consciousness.

Her head snapped up. She stared at Melvin, wild-eyed but aware. Stunned into a state of imbalance, he nearly fell back, nearly fell out of her. But he stabilized himself and avoided toppling. For a moment, the two were there as one – he, kneeling with his hand inside of her body; her, shuddering from shock as the son she never wanted was a part of her once more.

They stared into each other's eyes. He saw the hatred he had seen his entire life. He saw the pain that she had caused him. He saw nothing that would make him regret what he was doing. He smiled at her as she lost consciousness again. He hoped she would take the image of that smile with her to the depths of Hell where she belonged.

Pulling back, sliding his arm through an obstacle course of organs, he withdrew his empty hand. With it gushed spouts of blood. He grabbed at the knife on the floor, only picking it up and securing it after three attempts due to his hand being shaky and soaked. He pushed his knife wielding hand all the way into her. With both haste and great care, he cut at the blockage until he had made an opening. Withdrew the knife. He then reached into her with his bare hand. All the while he was certain he would be too late, that she would be dead before he was done. But the tough old bitch was still breathing when he wrapped his fingers around the faintly beating object in her chest.

It was large, dense, thick, a rubbery ovoid mass of muscle throbbing in his fist. The feeling of it, of all of this, repulsed him. But he fought against that disgust, focused instead on the sound of his meowing cat behind him, and the twisting, turning, tugging necessary to wrench the still-beating heart from his mother's chest.

Noises escaped his mother when he finally removed her heart. A noise from her nose as her last air left her. From her lower portion, the escape of gas and feces, the sound of releasing urine. But none of that – the sounds, the smells, the fact that he now had a corpse to get rid of – truly mattered. What mattered was the object still thrumming lightly in his blood drenched hand. And who it now belonged to.

"You hungry, little Lucy? You hungry?" he asked, turning to the table. She began to meow uncontrollably, the way she once had when he would rattle a bag of treats at her, or when he teased her with a ball of catnip before allowing her to pounce on it. But she couldn't pace and hop around the way she had back then, couldn't chase after him to get her prize. Her limbs were still too weak, so he brought the heart to her.

He knelt next to the table upon which she sat. With both hands, he presented his mother's heart to his cat. And watched, breath held, pulse pounding, as Lucy crawled her way to the table's edge to meet him, to obtain her long awaited meal.

Melvin had to fight off tears of joy as he watched his cat begin to eat.

19

Lucy was sleeping on the table, satiated and purring serenely, half her head red from gorging on Moira Cockburn's heart. Already her fur looked fuller, she looked heavier. Better.

Melvin was now sitting at the table across from his deceased mother, a smile on his face as he leaned back and watched his cat snoozing soundly, both of his hands dangling by his sides. Both of his hands dripping blood upon the floor.

He thought he could do a pretty good imitation of Lucy by falling asleep right then and there, exhausted as he was from his exertions, from the effort it had taken to feed his cat. He might have slept, but he realized that he couldn't. Not yet. He remembered that there was something else he had to do; the last thing he had promised his mother. It was something he had to deal with even before mopping the floor and cleaning up what looked like gallons of blood sprayed all over the kitchen.

Staring at the back door, into the back yard, Melvin wasn't exactly looking forward to what was next.

He still had to take care of Obi, the neighbour's dog.

20

Melvin was kneeling again. This time in front of a dog instead of his cat. The dog was restless. Antsy. But he held onto Obi's collar, his fingers tucked beneath it, between leather and fur, to make sure Obi didn't squirm or run away. Not until Melvin did what he had to do.

"Don't worry, little guy," he promised. "Everything's gonna be okay."

He couldn't wait for this to be over.

A sound caused him to stand. The door he and Obi were crouched in front of was opening. Inside the frame of that door was his neighbour, Mrs. Chloe Thames.

"Melvin? Obi! Oh, Obi, you're such a bad dog! Have you been in the Cockburn's yard again?" Mrs. Thames said to Melvin and her dog, opening her front door several minutes after he had rung the bell. He had known it would take her a while to answer the door. The woman's foot was broken, and she was in a walking boot.

He felt sorry for Mrs. Thames. Not only because of this recent injury of hers but because of each injury life had dealt her previously. Every time he saw her he was reminded that maybe his own miserable existence wasn't so bad. Reminded that he didn't know true loss and pain.

She looked older than she had the last time he'd seen her. And that had only been a month before, when he had been walking home from one of his many trips to the vet, and she had been sitting on her porch, reading a novel. He hadn't seen her up close then. Now, under her porch light, only two feet in front of her, he could see her thick black hair had a few more greys in it than he remembered, her almond coloured skin was paler than he recalled. And when she smiled at him apologetically, he thought he saw crow's feet extending from the corners of her eyes. Still, she was a pretty lady, and he was always nervous being this close to one of those. Which was why he stood there anxiously, waiting eagerly for this reunion between owner and animal to be over so he could get back to his house, his cat. His mother's corpse.

"Oh, no, Mrs. Thames, Obi was no problem."

"Is that true, Obi? Were you a good dog?" She had been speaking sternly to the dog she had named after a character from Star Wars since opening the door, and appeared genuinely embarrassed by his constant truancy, but there was still love and humour in her voice. And soon there was a smile on her face as Obi, sensing that he had gotten away with misbehaving again, lunged at Mrs. Thames, hopping up on his hind legs, his forepaws against her thighs in his joy at being back with his owner.

Mrs. Thames couldn't help but laugh, to which Obi responded with barking laughter of his own, furiously wagging his tail, clearly understanding he was off the hook once Mrs. Thames began rubbing his head and scratching him behind the ears.

Melvin found himself laughing as well. The joy of an animal, he understood, was infectious. And it was a joy Mrs. Thames sorely needed.

"I'm so sorry, Melvin. I'd keep him in the house more, but you've seen him, he tears the place apart if I don't let him run round in the yard for a few hours. Especially since we can't go out for our walks at the moment." She indicated her walking boot. "Was your mother upset?"

The mention of his mother made Melvin's pulse quicken. Caused him to stop laughing. He pictured her taped to the chair in the kitchen, blood all around her, the remnants of her heart – some fascia, a few valves, pieces of artery – on the kitchen table beside the cat that had consumed the rest of it.

"She was," he answered honestly. "She threatened to call the pound."

The joy in the little vestibule leading to Mrs. Thames's house seemed to evaporate with those words. She took a sharp inhale. Melvin knew how much the dog meant to her. Knew what losing Obi would have done to this already unfortunate woman.

Until two summers ago, there had a been a Mr. Thames. And a young boy, Devon Thames, ten years old and one of the nicest kids in the neighbourhood. He was one of the few people who didn't snicker at Melvin when he took Lucy for a walk on her leash around the block. Melvin attributed this to Devon being raised by a kind and caring woman. A woman whose life had turned upside down when the family of three had gone on a brief vacation.

Melvin had heard the loose details of what had happened from his mother, who treated the news like any piece of gossip, almost smiling when she mentioned the fate of Mr. Thames and Devon. Melvin got the rest of the details from the television the next day. From a reporter speaking with far more gravity than his mother had.

The Thames family had gone out for a boat ride near a cottage they had rented at Blue Sand Beach, a town that was a two-hour drive north of Saturn City. A place Melvin had only ever heard bad things about. It had been a serene and peaceful day, according to the news reporter. The Thames boy and a friend of his had been out in the water, life jackets on them, boogie boards beneath them. Mrs. Thames and her husband had been talking and eating on their boat, watching their son and his friend have the time of their lives.

Mrs. Thames and others in the area would later say that the boys had suddenly gone under the water. But it was not as though they were playing and had fallen from their boards or had simply submerged themselves for a swim; eyewitnesses had said that it seemed as if the boys had been snatched off their boards. Pulled in from below. Both of them yanked under in an instant nearly simultaneously.

Mr. Thames had jumped into the water, had swum to where his son had been, and had also been pulled under. Mrs. Thames, not a strong swimmer, had been screaming to those on the beach to help when her boat was crashed into from below. She found herself in the water under the boat, struggling to breathe.

She had told the authorities that the last memory she had before blacking out was of drowning. Her first memory, upon waking, was of coughing up water on the sand. Shortly thereafter she had been told that neither her son, his friend, nor her husband could be found. And they never had been.

Mrs. Thames had survived whatever freak occurrence had transpired under the water that day only to come home to an empty house, a broken life, a bleak future.

Melvin recalled that she had gotten Obi not long after. During those dark days, he would often see her taking long aimless walks with the little dog. He had figured that this was her way of coping with her losses, as had everyone who knew her. Which was why the neighbours didn't mind that the dog got loose from time to time. Obi was harmless and was an important part of a kind, unfortunate woman's healing. Everyone understood that. Everyone except for Melvin's mother. Thankfully, she wouldn't be bothering the dog anymore. And Obi could do what he wanted with her stupid flowers as far as Melvin was concerned.

"But don't worry," he added after seeing the distress on Mrs. Thames's face upon hearing about Melvin's mother's threat. "You won't have to stress about her at all. My mom and I had a serious heart to heart, and Obi was the reason for it. He's been a *very* good dog."

"Thank you *so* much, Melvin. Obi and I really appreciate it. And I'll make sure to head over and apologize to your mother right away. I know she's not very fond of him," the woman said worriedly as she patted an excited and oblivious Obi on the head.

"Oh no, Mrs. Thames! No need for that!" Melvin said. Then, hoping she hadn't heard the panic in his voice, he tempered himself, explained, "My mom is not the most chill person. I had to take the phone from her to stop her from calling the pound on Obi after he got into her petunias. It took *a lot* of convincing. If you went over there, she would just get annoyed all over again. Then who knows what she'd do? It's best to leave well enough alone when it comes to her. Besides, you ought to stay off that foot of yours. I already feel bad having you answer the door unexpectedly like this."

He felt bad for her in general. After all the emotional damage Mrs. Thames had endured with the loss of her husband and son, it seemed cruel for life to give her this sort of physical pain as well.

He had noticed the crutches beside her the last time he had seen her. The day she had been reading on the porch. When he'd stopped to ask if she was okay, she had told him about being in a bad car accident. Someone had fallen asleep, drunk at the wheel, and had driven directly into the back of her car going eighty kilometers an hour in a sixty kilometer an hour zone. She had subsequently been driven into the car ahead of her, creating a sandwich made of metal with Mrs. Thames as the meat.

The accident had resulted in a totaled car, whiplash, gashes, bumps, bruises, and a broken ankle.

When he had asked if she would be okay, she had laughed – a sound tinged with sadness – and said,

"Yeah, I've been through worse." Mrs. Thames was a true survivor.

"You're too sweet, Melvin. Thank you. Really. But how many times do I have to tell you, you don't have to call me Mrs. Thames! You can call me Chloe. We're practically the same age!" she said with a small chuckle that crinkled the corners of her eyes, emphasizing the kindness in them.

It was true, they were practically the same age. Melvin may have been a year older. But circumstances often outweigh chronology. While he might have been born around the same year as Chloe Anita Thames, he had stagnated by the time he had hit adulthood, his development arrested by a lack of progress, an absence of change and independence. He very much felt like the same lost adolescent he had been over twenty years ago.

He had spent those late teenage years sitting in his mother's basement, watching television, becoming further disconnected from society, while Mrs. Thames had left her home for college, had learned much, travelled the world, had become employed, fallen in love, gotten married, become a mother. She had felt the harsh, cruel, murderous hand of life and survived its blow. In terms of experience, she was far and away his senior. And because of those experiences, he looked up to her in a way that would not allow his mind to believe that they could be on the same level. She would always be Mrs. Thames to him.

Melvin patted Obi on the head, said, "You're welcome" to Mrs. Thames' many thanks, carefully avoided addressing her by any of her names, and left. He whistled on his way to a house filled with blood, occupied by the corpse of his mother.

At the thought of Moira Cockburn's mangled cadaver, he realized he would be independent for the first time in his life, no longer under his mother's thumb. No longer crushed by the heel of her boot.

Maybe this was the restart he needed after being in a state of hiatus for such a long duration. An unpausing of the game of life he had played so poorly. Maybe this was his opportunity to finally progress. Perhaps, he pondered, thinking of the possibilities in a world without his mother, he could one day feel comfortable with calling Mrs. Thames Chloe after all.

When he returned home, Melvin regarded his front door as though it were a portal to an alternate reality. A reality where he had just taken the life of the person who had given him his own. A world where he would have to spend the next several hours cleaning up her blood, vanishing her body. And praying he would never get caught for doing what he had done. That was his reality now.

"Worth it," he muttered, unlocking and opening the door. A sharp coppery smell assaulted his nose. With it was the smell of shit and puke. The cleaning, the burial of the body, the concern over being caught, it would all be worth it just to be rid of her and be with Lucy a little longer, Melvin reminded himself.

With that in mind, he ignored the stench of death that had overtaken his home, and walked into his house with a smile on his face, thinking of just how perfectly the day had gone.

21

Melvin had always hated cleaning. His mess of a basement was evidence of this. But he didn't mind it on this evening as he took wet towels to the floor of the kitchen to absorb the blood that was already partially dried. Next it was the mop and bucket to make sure he got it all.

With the television on and playing Much Music's weekly Top Thirty Countdown, Melvin practically danced with the mop as he cleaned the kitchen floor, delighted to see that Lucy was watching him as he worked, sometimes feeling bold enough to run up and swipe at the moving mop, believing this was a toy and her owner was playing some sort of game.

Just seeing her reaction made Melvin feel as though this was a game as well. He was elated that she had the strength to play. His mother's heart had worked, his cat was on the mend!

"Only good thing you've ever done," Melvin said to the corpse of his mother as it sat rotting at the table, taped to the chair, chest and belly open, chin drooping until it was practically inside of her vivisected torso.

After nearly three hours, the kitchen was devoid of blood. The innards that had fallen out of his mother had been collected and placed in garbage bags. He would dispose of those bags along with his mother's body, which was all he had left to do.

There was a shovel in the shed in the backyard, it was night, and he would have been covered by moonless dark had he felt like burying her. But he didn't feel like doing that. At least not tonight. He felt like keeping her there for now. He and Lucy had some celebrating to do, and he wanted his mother around as they did it.

22

The next morning was a disaster. At least it started out that way.

Melvin noticed that two things were wrong immediately upon opening his eyes. The first was what had woken him. The doorbell. An unexpected visitor. An unwelcome guest while his mother was still in the kitchen, a disembowelled blood covered cadaver.

He was in the living room adjacent to his mother's current resting place. He and Lucy had spent the night upstairs as owner of the house and his companion, cuddled together on the couch, enjoying the more comfortable seats and the larger environment. Melvin especially appreciated having an actual bathroom he could easily walk to rather than having to piss in the laundry room sink. He also appreciated the full-sized fridge that would be all his from now on.

The fridge, however, was empty. And that would turn out to be the reason for this morning's trouble.

He might have been upset about the empty fridge the night before, but his stomach had been acting up. After coming home from returning Obi to Mrs. Thames, not long after cleaning up the kitchen, Melvin had thrown up several times.

The thought of eating was one he hadn't entertained after that. If he had considered eating, he might have contemplated more carefully the lack of food inside the fridge, and what it would mean for him the next day. But that hadn't been at the forefront of his mind.

After he had finished mopping, had cleaned himself up, he and Lucy had watched movies on Moira's big screen. In colour rather than the black and white (or sometimes green) broadcaster of static he was familiar with downstairs. It had been one of the greatest nights of his life. But now it was morning, and everything might be about to crumble.

The doorbell sounded again.

Ignoring it, Melvin noted the second thing that was wrong that morning: Lucy appeared languid again.

She was no longer on the couch but on the floor under the coffee table. Before he had fallen asleep, she had almost been her old self again, hopping onto his lap when he had sat down, purring, raising her head for scratches like she often would before the cancer. Now she was laying on the carpeted floor, unmoving. The doorbell usually got a reaction from her, even when they were all the way downstairs. But this morning it was like she couldn't hear it.

Not a great sign.

He had known she would need more life. But he'd had no idea she would need it so soon.

The doorbell once more, followed by a knock, then a voice, barely audible:

"Ms. C? You okay in there? I've got your groceries!"

"Shit!" Melvin whispered harshly.

It was Brian, his mother's helper and errand boy. A college kid who had lived on their street until the previous year. Melvin's mother had been giving him twenty dollars a week to pick up and drop off her groceries over the last several months, ever since she had failed the province's mandatory Senior Driver's Licence Renewal test – a requirement of drivers eighty years of age and older – and was deemed too old to be a trustworthy motorist. It had been a bitter birthday present for Moira, and she had lashed out at Melvin terribly for weeks upon receiving the news, treating her son as though he had been the one responsible for her aging and inability to safely drive. But her errand boy, Brian had helped her adjust to life as an unlicensed senior, volunteering to drive her to appointments and to get her groceries for a fee when she had told him of her predicament.

Melvin had never gotten his licence. Despite there being a car parked in their garage, he had never been allowed to drive it. Whenever he had talked about driving as a teenager, Moira's response had usually been the same.

"Why?" she would say. "You don't have any friends. You don't have anywhere to be." Then she would laugh, as though the idea of him driving was the punchline to a joke.

"Bitch," he said to his mother's corpse as he made his way from the living room into the kitchen, debating if he would make the trek to the door to open it.

"Ms. C? You okay?"

"One second!" Melvin cried out. He had considered saying nothing, allowing Brian to go away. But the young man had to have been at the house recently to get the grocery money and list his mother provided him with each week. If she didn't answer now, he wouldn't just leave, he would worry. He was already worried based on the last words he had said.

Even if Brian went away, he would call the house upon returning to his home. And if Moira didn't answer, Brian's next call would be to the police, letting them know his eighty-year-old former neighbour and casual employer was likely injured or dead inside her home, with her lazy son in the basement witless of her dire circumstance.

Melvin couldn't have that.

"One second!" he shouted again.

Taking a deep breath, attempting to steady himself on legs that seemed at odds with the rest of him, not quite working the way his mind was commanding them to function, he walked shakily through the kitchen. And prepared himself to get rid of the nuisance at his door.

23

"Hey Brian," Melvin said after opening the door, attempting to sound both cheery and nonchalant. Failing twice.

"Melly? I'm surprised to see you." He looked at Melvin with open disdain as he spoke, two brown paper bags of groceries in his arms, cradled close to his body like the footballs he had been accustomed to carrying as a star of the sport in high school. "Is your mom around?"

Brian was a good-looking kid, tall, lean. An every sport kind of athlete who put non-athletes like Melvin to shame simply by existing. He was the type of jock who knew he was a jock and did all he could to fit the role. Currently, he wore a baseball cap backward on his head. On his body were blue jeans a size too big, and a white t-shirt covered by a Winston Saturn Collegiate Institute Letterman jacket. Winston Saturn C.I. was the high school Melvin had graduated from four years before Brian had been born. The jacket was a reminder of the bullies who had tormented Melvin during his teenage years.

Behind Brian, on the driveway, was a silver Honda Civic waxed to a sheen. Brian had purchased the vehicle the year before, having scrimped and saved to buy it since becoming a teenager, according to Moira.

The kid was a hard worker, Melvin's mother had often told him. He worked full time at the nearby Blockbuster Video while doing odd jobs when he could. All while going to school and playing sports. She had rubbed it in his face that Melvin was the opposite of the young man. Had said that, if he had shown the same initiative, even once in his life, that Brian showed on a regular basis, he might have done something with himself. Might have become more than the loser basement dweller that he was.

He knew she had shared that same sentiment with Brian, letting him know how lazy her son was, portraying herself as a helpless victim ignored by her unappreciative spawn. And for that reason, Brian didn't like him, and made no effort to hide it. Worse yet, Brian didn't respect him, which was the reason he was attempting to shoulder past Melvin and enter the house even before Melvin could think of an excuse as to why his mother wasn't answering the door.

"Hey!" Melvin said, speaking with more authority than he had ever spoken with before. "No one said you could come in. My mom's trying to sleep."

He stepped back from the doorway and centered himself directly in front of Brian, blocking him from getting any further into the house.

Brian stopped, likely more because of Melvin's statement than the blockade he had made of his body. The younger man's face showed surprise. Melvin would have seen surprise on his own face, too, if he'd had access to a mirror. Standing up to people wasn't exactly his strong suit.

"Your mom is expecting me... Jesus, what's that smell?"

"Smell? I don't smell anything." And he didn't. He had gone noseblind to the smell of his mother's corpse and all that had fallen out of it after spending a night only feet from her, like a person who didn't notice the stink of their own sweat. But, he supposed, to someone who had just entered from the fresh outside air, the place might smell like warm raw meat and shit. Like death and things decaying. "Anyway," Melvin added. "My mom is asleep."

"Asleep? She's never once been asleep when she's expecting her groceries. You sure everything's okay?"

Brian shot him a skeptical look. Then looked up the stairs before eventually letting his eyes drift over Melvin's shoulder in the direction of the kitchen. Melvin's heart accelerated, he could feel his armpits begin to leak. He did all he could to stop his body from visibly trembling. He couldn't let Brian see what he had done to his mother.

"Yes, everything's okay. She's eighty, you know. She's bound to slow down sometime. Maybe you can come back later."

"Come back later?" Brian said in a tone that was an extended scoff. "I have her groceries here, Melly. They've gotta be put away now."

He hated being called Melly, and knew that this punk kid was using the nickname mockingly. This wouldn't be the first time he had heard Brian openly deride him.

There had been a snowstorm last winter. Melvin, as always, had paid the weather no mind. His mini fridge had been stocked, in the deep freezer there had been plenty of frozen dinners he could heat up in his microwave. He'd had his cat and his TV, the condition of the outside world was of no concern to him. As for shovelling the driveway, that was something his mother had always done. Until she had begun experiencing issues with her hip three years prior, and eventually had to undergo surgery. She had relied on Brian to clear the driveway for her ever since. It was the snow shovelling that had led to Brian doing other errands for Moira, including the grocery runs.

On the day of the storm, Melvin had been listening to sports talk radio. Something that was said about the Toronto Maple Leafs had riled him up so badly he'd felt compelled to call in and speak his mind... for the third time that day. When he'd picked up the phone, he had heard his mother on the line speaking to Brian, asking him when he could come and shovel the driveway.

"I'm sorry, Ms. C, I've barely got enough time to shovel my own driveway before I go to hockey."

"Hockey? In a storm like this?"

"Can't let the guys down, Ms. C."

"Bless your heart, Brian. If only my lazy son had even a bit of the integrity you have, I wouldn't have to be begging for someone to shovel my driveway. If it wasn't for this damn hip of mine..."

"I'm sorry, Ms. C. It gets me real mad that your son refuses to help you out. No excuse for an able-bodied man to act that way."

"Man?" Moira had replied, sounding incredulous. *"He ain't no goddamn man. What I have in my basement is an overgrown baby."*

Then the two of them had laughed heartily. Melvin had set down the receiver to the sound of their ridicule buzzing in his ears. As if determined to further insult Melvin, to make him look small, Brian had shown up after his hockey game to shovel the Cockburn's driveway.

Now, the ever-helpful young man was taking a step toward the kitchen, again attempting to blow past Melvin as though he wasn't there. Again, Melvin stepped in front of him, obstructing his path like a bouncer trying to prevent a persistent drunk from entering a party.

"Give me the groceries. I'll take care of them." He practically panted out the words, panic making him short of breath. Brian's skeptical expression twisted to something of disgust, annoyance, and – there it was again – mockery.

"What's going on, Melly? What don't you want me to see?" Brian chided, a meanspirited smirk apparent on his face as he glared at Melvin, puffing out his chest and shoulders, somehow growing bigger, taller, and more jock-like right before Melvin's eyes.

This time, when Brian attempted to step past Melvin, he didn't bother to stop the bullheaded young man. He knew he wouldn't have been able to stop him even if he tried. But it didn't matter because his mind was focused on other things. The memory of that phone call between his mother and Brian had reminded him of something else. Something that might help him.

"This damn hip of mine," his mother had said.

As Brian walked toward the kitchen, Melvin raced to the closet near the front door, hoping... praying... *Yes!*

It was barely visible, wedged in the corner, obscured by a curtain of coats and a mountain of shoes, but it was there. The cane his mother had been told by her doctors she would need for the rest of her days after her hip procedure. The cane she stubbornly refused to use since she had deemed herself recovered. For once, he was glad for her hard-headedness. What she hadn't wanted to use then would be of great use to him now.

He grabbed the wooden cane and turned back just in time to see Brian step around the corner into the kitchen. Just in time to hear him shout,

"Holy shit! Holy shit!"

His cries were followed by the sound of two bags of groceries dropping to the floor.

Melvin raced toward the kitchen at a dead sprint, nearly tripping over himself when he tried to stop his momentum.

Brian was in the middle of turning when Melvin finally reached him. Brian was in the middle of speaking when Melvin put the cane to use.

"You sick fuck! What the fuck have you do–"

The polished wood handle of the cane collided with Brian's turning cheek. Barry Bonds himself couldn't have swung it any better.

Melvin couldn't believe what was happening. What he had done, what he was doing. The surrealness of it seemed to decelerate the world. Made it so he processed what was happening in slow motion.

He distinctly saw Brian's mouth explode. Blood, saliva, teeth propelled from between his lips, the bottom one of which had burst. Some of what had erupted from Brian's mouth landed on the kitchen floor Melvin had cleaned the night before, some of it landed on Melvin's face, in his open, panting mouth.

The taste of blood on his tongue sped the world up again.

He spat, revolted. But even as he spat, he had begun to smile. Brian's eyes rolled back in his head. He fell to his knees, then forward onto his forehead, his ass sticking up and into the air as if it were being presented to a lover. As if he was waiting to be fucked.

Looking down at the unconscious Brian, a river of blood flowing from his face, Melvin realized that the cane had solved two of his problems:

No more snotnosed kid to mock him.

Much more life for his little friend.

Grinning now, blood and spit dripping from his chin, Melvin looked over to the living room where he could hear Lucy meowing excitedly. He made eye contact with his cat as she crept toward the kitchen, beamed at the sight of her. He was glad to see that she was moving again. Was thrilled to hear that she was making that sound she made which was specific to her hunger.

But what Melvin was especially happy about, as he stood and smiled lovingly at his pet, was that, at the moment, it seemed as though Lucy was smiling back.

24

"Hello, Brian," Melvin said when the young man began to regain consciousness. He had been standing in front of Brian for minutes since lifting him from the floor and sitting him down, propping him up. Each long hand around the clock was an agony as he waited for this moment.

Brian's eyes fluttered open with an effort, as though his eyelids had become heavier while he'd been blacked out and the muscles which worked them were lifting an unaccustomed weight. He squinted. Looked down at himself. Then, upon realizing he was sitting in a chair, naked and duct taped to it, he turned his eyes to Melvin's. Fear making his lids lighter, he opened his eyes fully. And Melvin was pleased to read the understanding in them.

"You should have just left when I told you to. But *nooooo*, you couldn't do that, could you? Tough guy like you, nice guy like you, super helpful guy that you are." The words were sarcastic, they came out through a sneer; the voice carrying them was steely. Hard. "I could have taken care of the groceries. But that wasn't good enough. You couldn't be bothered to listen to a loser like me, eh? You had to walk in for yourself. Why? Because you wanted to show my mom you were here? Because you just *had* to let her know that *you* were the one who brought in the groceries and put them away? Were you hoping for a tip? Or did you just want to make me feel small like you did with all your goddamn snow shovelling? Huh? How are you feeling about your decision now?"

Brian didn't respond despite not being gagged as Moira had been. Melvin saw no need for the sock, the strip of tape. Brian's mouth was badly broken. Too broken for yelling and screaming to be a concern. All he was capable of doing was gurgling, grumbling wetly, as he attempted speech but only succeeded in producing red drool and bubbles of blood from his battered lips. Melvin wondered what words were trapped inside those bubbles.

The cane had done a great deal of damage. The young man's jaw had shifted out of place, which had caused his mouth to hang open and askance. Inside of that mouth, several jagged shards of teeth protruded from bloody gums. Between and around those shards, some teeth were missing entirely. His bottom lip was split horizontally nearly the entire way across. Both lips were swollen, as though Brian was in the middle of an allergic reaction. Like a bee had landed on his lips and he had been made to kiss its stinger.

His mouth was mush. The words he attempted to get out of it were much the same. Eventually, though, Melvin was able to understand something Brian was mumbling in response to his taunting. He recognized two of the words and was disappointed to hear them.

"Fuck me?" he said, enraged. "Fuck *me?*" His tone grew lower, harsher. Guttural. "Fuck *you!*" he spat, an aggressive whisper inches from Brian's broken face.

The disrespect, Melvin thought. *They never quit* .

It was then he stepped aside, out of Brian's direct line of sight, allowing the young man to see what sat across from him at the opposite end of the kitchen table. Allowing him a close-up look at the corpse of Moira Cockburn.

Brian began to shake, to shift and slide in his chair as though he was attempting to rattle his way out of his constraints. Trying to somehow run away even though each of his limbs were taped and bound and made unusable.

"Settle down, Brian. It'll be over soon."

Brian's eyes followed Melvin's movement as he reached toward the center of the table. Between Moira and Brian were the knife and honing steel.

He picked them up, slashed one against the other, and simply looked at Brian until the young man put two and two together and found they equaled death.

He attempted to speak again, to scream, but the words were barely more than moans and mumbles. Though somewhere in those sounds, Melvin thought he heard a "don't," a "please," a "stop." Words that brought a smile to his lips.

Brian was sweating and crying and spitting; leaking from his forehead, his eyes, drooling from his mouth as he efforted to protest.

Unlike Moira, the regret in his eyes was clear, and Melvin ate it up as eagerly as Lucy had eaten his mother's heart. As eagerly as Lucy would eat this second heart if her meowing was any indication.

The cat approached the bound young man and sat next to his right foot. She looked from Melvin to Brian, crying to be fed. Melvin understood that, to Lucy, this part of things was the opening of a can of tuna, the sound of kibble falling and clinking in her bowl. His bound and bloodied body was reminding her of her hunger. Her meows were turning to growls. She wanted to eat, and she wanted to eat immediately.

Brian's eyes flew all over the place. From the cat to the knife in Melvin's right hand to the sharpening tool in his left to Moira's open chest. Those wide and panicked eyes scanned the room and landed on the back door. Melvin wondered if Brian thought help might suddenly come through it. Melvin wondered if the young man believed he would be saved. He supposed Brian was an optimist.

"Thank you for the food, Brian. I mean that. You brought exactly what Lucy needed."

Melvin stepped toward the young man in the chair, honing tool abandoned on the table, knife held out in front of him pointed at Brian's sternum, its blade gleaming beneath the kitchen lights. Brian, seeing now that this was truly going to happen, that there would be no one to save him, began to writhe, to buck, as though fault lines had shifted in the earth beneath him. His chair teetered one way, tottered the other, until he sent it toppling over.

He flew backward, dropped toward the linoleum, only stopping when the back of his head broke his fall. And his fall broke the back of his head, judging from the sound.

His head, the floor, they made a sound like a cleaver connecting with a coconut, cracking through its shell.

"Fuck," Melvin said when he realized what that sound meant. "Don't you die on me!" is what he added when he saw the pool of blood that had begun to leak from Brian's skull.

He fell quiet when Brian began to convulse. To seize. His legs and arms straining against the tape confining him, veins bulging at his neck, his forehead. His eyes were open but rolled back, all white and pink and veined. His tongue was doing its best to choke him as he involuntarily began to swallow it.

"No, no, no, no..." Melvin muttered, rushing toward Brian with his mother's knife. Lucy was howling now, screaming for him to hurry, to not waste such a hearty meal.

Melvin only paused for a moment when Brian's bladder released, shooting sprays of urine into the air, forcing Melvin to run through this golden shower like a child through a lawn sprinkler on a hot summer day.

With Lucy's urging, he ignored the hot urine he felt spraying against his stomach, his chest, his cheek. Brian's dick finally stopped spurting as Melvin bent over him.

He placed the tip of the knife onto Brian's sternum, went to cut in and then cut downward, to make a hole that would allow him to reach under the ribcage for the heart without killing the young man. But at that moment, Brian's body jerked violently, and the knife plunged deep into his torso.

"Nooo!" from Melvin.

A yowl from Lucy.

Seconds later, a sputtering sound from Brian as blood began to geyser out of his open mouth. Melvin had punctured his lung, and now Lucy's living meal was surrounded by a body that was choking on its tongue, drowning in its own blood, and bleeding out from both the head and body.

She hissed at Melvin to hurry, to salvage this thing before the heart stopped beating. And that was what Melvin intended to do.

Instead of kneeling next to Brian's twitching body, he knelt on it, straddling his shoulders while facing Brian's knees, pressing him down so he could steadily create the entry wound.

Brian spasmed and convulsed, making the task at hand difficult. But Melvin was determined, and soon he had cut through skin and muscle, had entered the wound and carved his opening, his tunnel to the heart. His pathway to Lucy's salvation. One large enough to fit his fist and forearm.

He hopped off the dying young man, knelt by his side to gain a better angle to obtain the prize he and Lucy so desperately needed.

In Brian's body past his wrist, his forearm, up to his elbow, he followed the light thrumming until he felt the beating heart. It was larger than his mother's and didn't yield as easily. When he tried to pull, the heart initially wouldn't budge. Melvin had to reach in further, nearly past it, fumbling around in the wet hot warmth of this young man's chest until he found what felt like connecting pieces of tissue that kept the heart rooted to the body.

He yanked. For an absurd moment he was reminded of a farmer wrenching a carrot from his field; a potato, a turnip, some root vegetable needed for nourishment. And Melvin thought of this as his harvest. Brian had sowed and now Melvin would reap, taking this living heart – this *life* – to feed his loved one.

He pulled violently until there was a wet popping noise, and the organ was released. The sudden lack of tension caused Melvin to fall backward out of Brian, landing hard on his shoulder, nearly crushing Lucy, who yelped and leapt out of the way.

But Melvin wasn't bothered by the hard landing, nor by his cat's theatrics. What mattered was that she was okay, and that, in his hand, raised toward the ceiling like a sacrifice to the Aztec Sun God whose name Melvin could never remember, he held a beating heart.

"Come here, Lucy. Come eat," he rasped.

She did as he requested, hurrying to the hand he had lowered toward her as he raised himself to a sitting position. By his side, Lucy began to devour the heart in his hand, ripping off sections of it, chewing and swallowing until it was no longer beating. At the same time, Brian's body stopped twitching, finally recognizing that it was dead.

Melvin dropped the heart on the floor. Barely waiting for it to fall, Lucy pounced on top of it. Attacking it. Making the same hideous, ravenous noises she had previously made when attempting to eat her own tumour.

Trying to ignore the sounds of his cat's desperate hunger, and the feeling that he might once again be sick, Melvin let loose a breath he had been holding for some time. Drained, he allowed himself to fall back onto the cool kitchen floor, his body landing with a soft thud, his bloody arm with a wet splat.

And as he lay there, exhausted, he couldn't help but wonder why being a pet owner had to be so difficult.

25

Melvin sat at the kitchen table. Lucy was in the seat to the right of him, asleep, purring noisily, appearing healthier and happier than she had been in months.

"Thank you, both of you, from the bottom of my heart," he said to the bodies taped into a seated position on the two remaining chairs around the small round table.

His mother's corpse sat across from him, her skin turning grey. Her head seemed to droop further toward the open cavity of her chest each time he looked at her, gravity and the weight of it making putty of her neck, stretching it little by little. In his mind was the grotesque image of her face falling inside of her own torso.

Brian's much fresher, far messier corpse had been righted from the ground and was to his left. His entire body was red.

"Thank you for saving my little Lucy," he clarified, looking from each of them to Lucy. Smiling at her.

"Look at us, huh? A little happy family. Who woulda thunk it?" Melvin clapped his hands happily and stood. "Well, I've got to take a little trip. But I'll be back, and we'll catch up. How's that sound?"

Neither of the corpses responded.

"I'll be back, Luce. You stay good, okay?" He rubbed her gently on the head. She shifted in the seat to nuzzle his hand, leaving flakes of semi-dried blood on his fingers and palm. "I'll have to clean you up when I get back."

She meowed softly and went back to sleep.

Feeling better than he had since the day he'd first found Lucy – the day she had saved his life – Melvin walked toward the front door, but first stopped in the bathroom to take one more look at himself in the mirror.

He wore a Winston Saturn Collegiate Institute Letterman jacket (something he had never received when he attended the school), a white shirt underneath. Outside of the range of the mirror, he wore a pair of jeans that were two sizes too large. On his head, covering his bald spot, was a baseball cap with the Saturn Shining Star minor league hockey team logo on it – a blue silhouette of the planet Saturn surrounded by a large yellow star. He, however, wore this hat the correct way, the brim low upon his brow, instead of backward, the way Brian had worn it. He looked the part, he thought, as he admired himself in Brian's clothes.

Could he have been a jock, an athlete, one of the cool kids if his mother hadn't told him how much of a loser he was his entire life? If she hadn't told him he was a retard, a mistake, something that should have been aborted, could he have been a boy like Brian?

"Yo," he said into the mirror, nodding as though he were addressing someone else. In his mind, he was AC Slater walking the halls of Bayside High; he was Dylan McKay, zip code 90210; he was the Fresh Prince in the kingdom of Belair. He was Arthur Fonzarelli, and this would be one of many Happy Days. "Ayyy!" he added, giving his mirrored self a thumbs-up as he chuckled, imagining a version of him that could have been.

Once upon a time.

"If not for that cunt," he said, glowering into the mirror, his mood going from bright to gloom in a matter of seconds. A shooting star felled.

But then he pictured his mother, strapped to a chair, her insides exposed, her life finally out of her old disgusting body, and he smiled. Then chuckled again, as if to prove he had gotten the last laugh.

Winking at the person in the glass in front of him, pointing two finger guns at the mirror and shooting them both, Melvin readied himself to be as cool and calm as he had ever been. As cool and calm as all of his television heroes.

It was time to take Brian's car out for a drive.

26

It was a strange sensation, driving through Saturn City. Driving at all.

Melvin had never gotten his licence, but there had been a time when that was all he had wanted. As a kid, he had loved the idea of driving, imagining a car as a mobile suit of armour that made a person, for a while, some hybrid of human and machine. He imagined it was the closest one could get to being a cyborg, the idea of which had greatly appealed to the child he had been.

Shortly after turning seventeen, despite his mother's urgings that he would never need a car, Melvin had gone for his driver's test and had failed it in spectacular fashion. His mother, upon hearing the news, had laughed before reminding him that he wasn't even smart enough to read, how could he expect to be allowed to drive? He had given up any hope of getting his licence after that.

His mother hadn't been entirely wrong. Melvin had always struggled with reading. When this issue had first emerged, and Melvin, along with his third grade teacher, had wondered why the young boy was behind the other students when it came to reading comprehension, Moira's response had been to say that her son had been born retarded. Probably because his father was a pig.

It had been one of the few times throughout his childhood that Moira had referenced the man who was fifty percent responsible for Melvin's creation. Him being a pig was the only detail about his father that Moira had provided her son for years prior to telling him the full story of his conception when Melvin had been fourteen and she had been stinking drunk and feeling particularly mean. Prior to that, whenever Melvin wanted to ask her to elaborate about his father, to further describe this estranged pig-dad of his, he remembered the time he had asked of his father before, and the claps he had received to the side of his head as a result. So, Melvin hadn't asked. He had accepted that his father was a pig. For a time, after he had rid himself of the silly notion of Moira being literally his mother and father, Melvin had imagined that his mom had actually lain down with a pig, and had caused him to be born more beast than boy because of it. He assumed that was the cause of all his issues; the reason he was slower than his classmates.

It wasn't until he had seen a TV documentary about dyslexia only a few years ago – well into his thirties – that he had realized what the root of his reading issue was. He wasn't retarded, the way his mother had described him all his life, he just had a learning disability. That was what had held him back all those years.

There was therapy for his condition, according to the documentary; training one might undergo to learn better, to help something Melvin had believed couldn't be helped. A teachable way to prove his mother wrong. He considered enrolling in the program described in the documentary. Briefly. But he figured it was pointless by then. Too late for anything to make a difference in his life. And too much work for what he didn't see as very much of a reward.

By then, he no longer dreamed of being a cyborg or anything else. He had long since lost all ambition and was content with simply living day to day until Death found him. He no longer had that childish interest in driving, in exploring. He was content with taking the bus to his few appointments or to the grocery store, which was only two kilometers away. He had no friends or loved ones to drive to – his mother had been right about that. When he needed to escape, he turned on his television, and was able to remove himself from this world and be part of so many others. Others where he wasn't a loser, an outcast. That was why he had decided not to take those classes. There had been no need for change or self-improvement. Melvin's life was set.

But now, on this late summer morning, he was out in the world, driving, cruising. The only thing ruining this surreal experience was his worry that he might see flashing lights behind him, hear the warning whoop of a siren followed by the amplified voice of an officer asking him to pull over. His concern was that he would be questioned, grilled, arrested for double homicide, and further charged with matricide. And he couldn't have that.

Who would take care of Lucy?

It was for those reasons – his concern for his freedom and for Lucy's survival – that Melvin fought the urge to take a detour, to drive around the city as though he had no cares in the world. Instead, he drove as fast as he legally could from his home to his destination.

This wasn't the first time he had driven despite never having been licensed. Over the years, his mother had, a time or two, vacated from their home. Moira had taken a bus trip across the border to Pennsylvania for a weekend of shopping when Melvin had been in his early twenties. That had been a particularly significant departure.

It was then he had taken her car for the first time. Had driven it slowly and carefully around the block, then around the neighbourhood, fighting off the nervous voice in his head screaming at him to go back home the entire while.

When he had gotten home, his excitement, his arousal, had been so great, he had spent the next seven minutes or so rifling through, then stickying, the pages of that month's *Beaver Hunt* magazine.

Two years later, his mother had taken another short trip with a man she had been dating for a brief period. Feeling slightly less nervous about it on this occasion, Melvin had driven himself to the southern and most dangerous part of Saturn City. Down by the harbour to a part of the city called Coal Town, where there had once stood several essential factories, including the Saturn Power Station, the infamous coal plant which had eventually leeched toxins into the city's water supply and poisoned half of its residents. That had been decades ago. Since then, the area had been turned to a low-income housing community. And a part of it had taken on a less than flattering reputation, being referred to as 'Hooker Harbour' by most people familiar with that portion of the city.

Those who knew of the area generally stayed away from it. But that was where Melvin had driven to when he had taken his mother's car. And that was where, in the back seat of his mother's car, he had finally lost his virginity after twenty-five years of living. Barely.

He had only just thrust his condom-covered penis into the thin, dry, and dusty looking street walker when he had ejaculated. After regaining control of his shuddering, spasming body, he had nearly cried from embarrassment, apologizing profusely to the prostitute.

She had simply readjusted her skirt and smiled, said, with the slurring accent of the consistently inebriated, "Don't worry about it, kid. Happens all the time. 'Sides, I don't get paid by the hour." Then she had taken his fifty-dollar bill and left the car without another word.

He had tried again with prostitutes twice after that. Reaching out to both via conspicuous advertisements in the Yellow Pages. He had agreed to meet with one at a motel in Hooker Harbour called The Sleep Easy Motel – known colloquially in Saturn as The Sleasy. He had taken the bus there for an experience that had lasted five minutes instead of barely one. He did it again the following month, this time experiencing a whole eight minutes of sex, the entirety of which had consisted of him sweating over a hooker who had lain there unmoving. She had been so drug addled she was practically unconscious. Both the sex and what had happened after were far less pleasurable than they had been with the previous prostitute.

Before he could leave the motel property, he had been surrounded by street toughs, members of one of Saturn's many gangs, and robbed at knife point.

In the end, the following had been taken from him in addition to the hundred dollars he had spent on the motel room and his brief pleasure: sixty dollars and fifty-five cents (money he had been saving, bit by bit, for years), his shoes, one of his only dress shirts, his belt, and his desire to ever solicit sex again.

Since then, the only sex he'd had was with his hand as he flipped through pages of the *Swank* or *Juggs* or *Leg Show* magazines he still kept hidden under his bed. Occasionally, he would rent an adult video at the corner store in the neighbourhood next to his.

Now, he had that itch again. It was likely because he was dressed as Brian, driving a hip car, feeling young and cool, Brian's rap music playing low from the speakers, the window rolled down, the late morning air blowing over him.

All of it was making his dick hard. And he wanted to do something about that.

But he didn't. He couldn't. He stuck to the plan.

Melvin drove to Saturn City Center, which, by late morning, was teeming with people all in a rush to do something, buy something, or go somewhere.

Most of them wouldn't notice this car pulling into the packed parking lot. Most of them wouldn't register the man in the baggy clothes, and the hat pulled low over his brow exiting the car, leaving it there. But Melvin was sure that if someone did notice him, they would give the police Brian's description, and the police might simply believe the young man had come here, abandoned his vehicle, gone to the bus terminal connected to the mall, and travelled somewhere for a new adventure.

A new adventure, Melvin thought, removing Brian's hat and jacket when he felt he was far enough from Brian's car, away from the busy parking lot and out of sight of any curious eyes. A new adventure is what he felt like he was on even as he walked toward the familiar bus terminal connected to the mall he had visited all his life. He tossed the hat and jacket in a trash bin he had placed his refuse in countless times before.

It felt like a new adventure even as he boarded the same old bus to his same old house. Life felt different now, exciting, epic. Changed and charged. He only hoped that Brian's heart was enough to heal Lucy for good. And wondered, briefly, but long enough for the thought to temporarily cloud his good mood, what he would do if Brian's heart was not sufficient.

As he looked out the window of the moving vehicle, staring at the streets of Saturn, thinking of its citizens, he couldn't help but ask himself what he would do when Lucy became hungry again.

27

Three buses and a short walk after ditching Brian's car, Melvin was back on his street, nearly home. Rushing to get there. His primary concern, even with two corpses rotting in his house, was how his cat was doing.

There was only one sidewalk on his street, and it brought him to the house across from his before he crossed the road and headed home. It was the house that belonged to his obnoxious neighbours, the Gormans. And it always made him antsy to approach it.

Usually, he worried about the young, sexy couple making fun of him in their loud, drunken whispers. Today, he was concerned that they might see him in Brian's oversized shirt and baggy jeans, and somehow connect his ill-fitting apparel to Brian's disappearance. To his murder.

He was being paranoid, he knew, but he also knew that paranoia would be a constant part of his personality now that he had become a killer.

A killer, he shuddered at the thought. *Is that really what I am?*

Approaching the Gormans' house, he allowed the question to go unanswered, relief that his neighbours were not on their porch overtook his thoughts. He scurried across the road, knowing that he was fortunate to have avoided them while both leaving and returning.

Following him across the street and to his door was the smell of cooking meat and the din of loud, obnoxious, artificial sounding music coming from the Gormans' back yard, an indication to Melvin that they were having one of their frequent private parties. And not once did they ever invite him over for a burger or a dog. But he wouldn't allow that to ruin his mood. Not today. Not after he had achieved so much.

Upon entering his house, Melvin went straight to the kitchen, his heart racing as though expecting the two bodies to have stood up and disappeared. Or as if it might be possible that the police had already found out what he had done and would be by the table, waiting for him.

Paranoia, there it was again.

But his paranoia was unfounded, Melvin saw as he entered the kitchen. Both bodies were there. Still dead, open, and unmoving. And now he could smell what Brian had smelled when he had barged into this house.

After being out in the world, Melvin's nose registered the aroma of rotting flesh, the fecal fragrance of what he knew was smeared between his victim's bottoms and the seats they were taped to. He could smell their dried blood. But he found that he didn't mind any of these odours. This was a potpourri that spoke of his victory. His freedom. His cat's improving health.

"Hey guys!" Melvin said to the corpses with a smile and a wave. This was the happiest he had ever been to see either of them. They, of course, did not return his greeting.

He tossed both his and Brian's keys on the kitchen table between his mom and her helper, the latter set of which he would have to bury with their bodies. Something he was dreading. The digging, the moving of bodies, the covering of them with the dirt he had dug; it would be a more physically draining task than anything he had done in his life. And he was already worn down from having to drag and prop Brian's body in the chair that morning. From having to navigate through Brian's twitching torso and retrieve his heart. But he would worry about digging their shared grave later. For now, all he cared about was seeing Lucy.

He found her on the couch in the living room. She was sleeping soundly. To his relief, she still looked as strong as she had when he had left. He hated that he would have to disrupt her, but it was time to change her garments.

It was time to face the tumour.

Melvin went downstairs to get the menstrual pads and change of onesie he always dreaded. When he returned to the living room, he found that Lucy was no longer sleeping, but was standing up on the couch, as if waiting for him. As if knowing this terrible process was upon them once again.

She fussed, swiped at him a time or two, but was unusually patient as he undressed her and removed her makeshift bandages to look at her malignancy.

"Wow!" Melvin exclaimed. The abscess had gotten smaller. The lump had shrunken by half. And the festering opening in the middle of it was smaller too, as though it were closing. More evidence of her healing.

When he finished changing her, he ran to the kitchen to tell the corpses the wonderful news. They, however, seemed indifferent to this information.

"Of course you wouldn't be happy for me," he grumbled darkly at his mother before immediately perking up. "But you won't be here for long. It's almost time for you and Brian to move into your new home."

28

Melvin waited until the sun had set to bury them. He had spent the day in the living room sitting feet from the two corpses, watching football and baseball with Lucy on his lap when she wasn't roaming around the house, stopping periodically to sniff at Brian and Moira. As soon as night descended, he walked to the back yard, a smile on his face despite the arduous task ahead of him.

Using the tools from her shed, he carefully uprooted his mother's precious petunia plants and dug for hours until he had created a hole of a decent depth and width below where they had been planted. A grave large enough for two bodies.

Cutting the bodies from the chairs was far easier than taping them to the chairs had been. But it was a far more revolting process. Melvin had braced himself for a mess, but he hadn't been prepared for the excess of loose feces and inexplicable bodily excretions that was left behind on the seats his mom and former neighbour had occupied. Doing his best not to vomit (as he had again earlier that afternoon), Melvin had wrapped both bodies in the sheets that had been on his mother's bed. He had needed to change the sheets anyway since the bed would be his from now on.

He dragged their bodies to the yard, rolled them into the hole he had made in it, buried them facing each other in their linen shrouds, and replanted the petunias atop their corpses. Then, he had urinated on the grave before going inside to clean and shower.

The entire ordeal took him most of the night. It was nearly morning by the time he was out of the shower. His aging bones ached, he was feeling weary, and, as had been the case for the last few days, he felt sick to his stomach. The bodies, bodily fluids, the burial; it was enough to make Melvin throw up again, this time in the toilet in the bathroom connected to his new fancy bedroom.

Afterward, he barely had the energy to dress his new bed, but was encouraged when Lucy joined him, jumping all over the sheets, winding up under them as he tried to put them in place. She did this every time he changed his sheets, and it never failed to make him laugh. He laughed now even as he nearly cried, the sight of her so lively made a mess of his emotions.

After securing the bedsheet to the mattress, he had fallen onto it exhausted but happy with Lucy snuggled up beside him. They stayed that way, coverless and pillowless but content, his arm over her, her purring as he provided her with warmth.

It took Melvin longer than expected to fall asleep considering how mentally tired, how physically exhausted, and how happy he was to be with a healing Lucy. His mind was still racing. Paranoia again.

He tried to relax, attempted to push away the negative thoughts, to focus on the new adventure he was now fully immersed in. New room, new circumstances. New him. He was finally the man of the house. He was finally a man.

But, as exciting as that seemed, he had to wonder how this adventure might end, hoping it wouldn't be inside some cell for what he had done to Brian and his mother. He couldn't bear the idea of going through all of this, doing all he had done, only to be torn away from Lucy at the end. That would be a fate too cruel to handle. The thought of it was enough to make him shiver.

He pulled the covers up to his nose, as he always did when he had nightmares or nightmarish ideas, and instead thought happier thoughts. Baseball. Boobs. He thought of things that made him smile.

HUMANE SACRIFICE

Finally drifting to sleep, Lucy snug beside him, Melvin hoped he had done enough to ensure he would never hear from the police when someone inevitably declared Brian missing.

29

Melvin heard from the police the very next morning.

He and Lucy had slept through the night. They would have slept into the afternoon if not for the phone ringing, an alarm clock that could not be snoozed. But Melvin attempted to do just that. He reached over with an arm that felt as though weights had been strapped to it overnight, his limb like the limb of a large tree, heavy and stiff due to yesterday's exertions.

He retrieved the receiver from the cradle but had no intention of answering the call. He hung the phone up immediately as he heard Lucy, startled by the ringing and the movement of her owner, scurry from the room. Confident she would be back, he rolled over and attempted to return to slumber.

His eyes had barely closed before the phone rang again.

Melvin growled, slapped the mattress in annoyance. Groggily, he reached for the phone for a second time. On this occasion, the receiver made it to his ear.

"Hello?" Melvin said, hearing and feeling the sleep in his voice, as well as the agitation at having been woken up and parted from his cat. He shifted on the sheets until he was propped up on one elbow, wincing with every movement. He was sore because of Brian and his mother. His mother, who the person on the line was calling to speak to.

"Hello? My name is Detective William Kelly with the Saturn City Police Department. I was hoping to speak to a Mrs. Moira Cockburn." The man's voice sounded like a lifetime of cigarettes and coffee.

Melvin was fully awake now. Had gone from feeling like he could hibernate to being hyperalert in a matter of moments. With his mind cleared of sleep there was space now for a flashback to the murder of his mother, a recollection of how he had butchered Brian. Remembrances of digging both their graves. Along with those memories came an imagining as clear in his mind as the events that had already happened, as clear as inevitability: Melvin in handcuffs being led to a police cruiser from his home by this detective on his phone.

"Ms...." Melvin responded instinctively, not sure why he had said it. Perhaps it was because he didn't know what else to say. Was too scared to think properly. And was also annoyed. "And it's Co-burn. Not Cock-burn." He wasn't making things any better for himself, but he couldn't help it.

"Pardon?" replied the detective.

"Co-burn is how our last name is pronounced. And *Ms.* is what my mom liked to be called. She was never married. She hated being called Mrs."

Melvin's mother had nearly snapped every time she was referred to as such. Each time he heard the word 'Mrs.' he thought of his mother's reaction.

"*Liked? Hated?*" the detective said, keying in on Melvin's poor phrasing. "I'm sorry, is *Ms. Co*-burn no longer with us?"

"No, no, no, no," Melvin replied. Too strongly, too urgently. He did his best to calm his system, wishing he could think clearly, wondering how his heart had managed to leave his chest and move up inside his skull, sharing the space with his brain, drumming loudly, drowning out his thoughts. "I mean, no she's *not* no longer with us, but she's not with us right now... I mean, she's away on a trip. What I meant by 'hated' is that I haven't heard anyone call her 'Mrs.' in years."

There was a pause from the person on the other end of the phone. In the silence between them, Melvin could hear what sounded like a pen scribbling against a pad of paper.

"I see... And you are?" asked the lawman.

"I'm Melvin Cockburn. Her son."

"Does your mother usually take trips the day after ordering her groceries?"

Fuck, Melvin thought.

"Pardon?" Melvin said.

"I'm calling about a former neighbour of yours. A young man named Brian Norton. He was reported missing early this morning. According to his girlfriend, he was supposed to deliver groceries to your mother, meet up with a study group at Verndale Comunity Center, and then meet her for a date. Except he never showed up for either their date or his study group. That leaves the grocery run. Did you happen to see Brian yesterday at any point?"

"Oh... Wow... I hope he's okay... No, I didn't see him at all. I live in the basement, and I don't really get involved with what my mother is up to. I thought I heard her talking to someone who sounded like it *could* have been Brian, but I didn't see him."

"Was it typical of him to stay and talk to your mother after bringing her groceries?"

"Ummm... I guess? They're kinda weirdly close for an old woman and a kid..." Melvin said, hoping the officer picked up on the suggestion.

"I see..." More scribbling of pen on pad. "And now they're both nowhere to be found. Did your mother mention where she went yesterday?"

"She mentioned visiting a sick friend in Montreal," Melvin said without a pause, proud of himself for thinking so quickly. "She's gettin' up there, you know. Lots of sick friends when you get to her age." Except his mother didn't have any friends. And she certainly didn't know anyone in Montreal that Melvin was aware of. Feeling proud about the lie only seconds ago, he now wondered if adding that detail was a mistake. The detective's next response confirmed to him it was.

"Does she have a phone number I could reach her at in Montreal? Brian's family is extremely worried. I'm hoping to put their minds at ease. It might help to know if he told her where he was headed."

Melvin began to perspire. He needed to think of the right response, but each second he took to answer felt like an eternity. During those everlasting moments, the breathing of this nosy cop sounded like Judgment Day come nigh.

"My mom is..." Melvin started speaking to break the silence, though he wasn't sure exactly how to finish the sentence. Then he decided to go with the truth. "...kind of a crank. I don't think she'd like having her sick friend's number given to anyone, espccially a cop. She doesn't much like the police. No offense. Tell you what? If you give me your info, I'll break the news about Brian to her gently, and I'll see if there's anything she knows. If there is, I'll try my hardest to get her to call you. Is that okay?"

This time it was the detective who took several seconds to answer, and when he did, Melvin didn't much like the tone of his voice.

"I see... Thank you, Mr. Cockburn. I'm sure we'll be in touch. I may have a few more questions for you depending on how things turn out." Then he provided Brian with his title and name for a second time, his precinct number, badge number, and phone number. Information Brian didn't bother to write down.

"No problem at all, Detective Kelly. Good luck finding Brian," Melvin said before returning the receiver of the phone to its cradle. He fell back onto his mother's bed, shaken.

"No problem at all..." he repeated to himself. That had been the largest lie he'd told the investigator. It felt as though Melvin suddenly had many problems, and no idea of how to solve them. The uncertainty of it all, the feeling that things were going to go wrong, seemed to impact Melvin physically.

His stomach began to burble. Scrambling from the bed, he ran to the bathroom.

30

Melvin barely made it to the toilet in time, starting to projectile vomit even as he was lifting the seat. Some of his ejection hit the lid and splashed back at him, causing him to vomit in his own face.

It lasted too long, is what Melvin thought when he finally stopped purging. His throwing up had seemed to last an impossible duration of time. Eventually, he found himself dry heaving, retching, sweating profusely, his muscles clenching and burning, his throat on fire, veins all over his body threatening to explode. And his eye, something was wrong with his eye.

He slumped against the toilet, his body sore, parts of it freshly throbbing from the effort of being sick. He wanted to stay there on the floor for the rest of the day, but he couldn't. Because his stomach grumbled again. Though this time in a different way.

Melvin scrambled up from the floor using the toilet for leverage with one hand as he pulled down his pants with the other. He attempted to sit on the seat, and nearly slipped off due to the vomit still on it. But he managed to sit down and settle himself in time to keep whatever dignity he felt he had left. The contents of his stomach – which Melvin had been certain were all voided – sprayed out of him again.

With his head in his hands, puke still wet upon his cheeks, chin, and chest, and shit pouring out of him in painful bursts like water from a rusty spigot, Melvin moaned before saying,

"What the fuck is wrong with me?"

31

"What the fuck is wrong with me?" Melvin said after moaning. This time while looking into the bathroom mirror.

He had peeled himself off the toilet after moving his bowels, and had gone straight to the shower, knowing that no amount of toilet paper would leave him feeling unsoiled.

Now, after showering, he stood in front of the mirror. Wiped it as clear as he could of steam. In the foggy glass he saw something that made him wince. He attempted to wipe the mirror further, but realized the reflection he saw was blurry not because of the steam, but because of his left eye. His left eye, where, straddling the pupil and spreading over the white of it, there was a large red blotch. He had vomited with such violent force that he had burst a blood vessel.

He released another groan. Looking from his eye to the rest of his face, he saw his skin was nearly grey. His hair seemed thinner than usual. He touched the top of his head, near the back. He couldn't be certain, but it felt as though his bald spot was spreading, forcing his hair to retreat down the back and sides of his head. He looked like he was recovering from two black eyes, the skin around them dark and wrinkled. Melvin appeared to have aged several years overnight.

"You're stressed out," he said to the haggard version of himself in the mirror. "This is all because you're stressed out."

And wouldn't anyone be stressed out in Melvin's situation? It wasn't every day a person committed murder. And here he had done it two days in a row.

While looking at his blood-burst eye, his gaunt and sallow cheeks, his downturned mouth, he heard Lucy meowing from somewhere downstairs.

Meowing hungrily.

Two murders... Melvin reflected to his reflection. The face that looked back at him was terrified. Because the sounds Lucy was making caused him to wonder if there would have to be a third.

32

"C'mon, Lucy. You used to love these!" Melvin cried, frustrated, as he continued to shake the bag of treats in his hand. Lucy only sat there on the kitchen floor next to the pantry cabinet, staring at him blankly before meowing in that certain way. Announcing she was hungry.

"I know you're fucking hungry. That's why I'm trying to get you to eat!" He hurled the bag of treats against the back door. The contents of the bag exploded out of it, sending a small storm of brown cat treats all over the kitchen. And subsequently sending a scared Lucy scampering from the room.

"Oh no! Lucy! I'm sorry! I'm just trying to get you to eat! Please come back!"

But he heard her little paws pattering down the stairs and knew she would be headed to some hiding place where he could never reach her. One she wouldn't come out of until she was good and ready.

Melvin, near to tears, sat down at the kitchen table, on the same chair his mother had sat on as he had slaughtered her. Where she had continued to sit for over a day after she had been killed.

He was sore, he was sick, he was upset. He had been trying to get Lucy to eat for several minutes.

After hearing her meowing from the bathroom, he had gone to retrieve her food from the basement. She had ignored the dry food entirely, and had gagged when he put a small dish of her old favourite wet food – chunks of turkey in gravy – under her nose. Then she had recoiled. Had leapt away from the food she used to love. After that, he had tried and failed with the treats. And now Melvin didn't know what to do.

Except he did know what to do. He knew exactly how to get her to eat, and the idea of it horrified him.

"Are we really considering this, Mel?" he said to himself, covering his face with his hands. "Are we going to go out and murder someone so that Lucy won't die?"

He didn't think he could do it. Didn't think that was who he was. Despite having killed two people, he didn't consider himself a murderer. Not really. With his mother, he had felt he had to stop her from getting sweet Mrs. Thames' dog put to sleep just for sniffing some flowers. Besides, that had been a long time coming.

And hadn't he tried to warn Brian away? Yes. Several times. He had told that idiot kid to leave, to go home. When his mother's errand boy hadn't listened, Melvin had been left with no choice but to do whatever it took to keep his secret, and his freedom. When he thought of it that way, killing Brian was practically self-defence. It just so happened that Lucy could take advantage of that unfortunate situation.

But could he actually go out and hunt a human being? Could he leave his house armed with the intent to kill?

He removed his hands from his face when he heard Lucy meowing. She was back in the kitchen, sitting on the floor next to his feet, staring at Melvin as if waiting for him to decide.

She looked better, he observed, though she didn't look quite like her old self yet. But she could be healthy again, he was sure of it. She had gained a bit of weight (though she was still too thin), her fur wasn't as limp and lifeless as it had been when he had come home from his most recent trip to the animal hospital. And he had seen the tumour for himself. It had improved! It was healing! That meant that if he fed her enough of what she wanted...

No, Melvin thought, shaking his head at the idea of it. Even if he was able to heal her, how much longer did she have left? She had practically been a kitten when he had found her, when they had saved each other. But he'd had her for twelve years since. How could he justify going out and killing a stranger just for another year or two of his cat's life?

Lucy meowed, long and loud.

Melvin looked at her. Their eyes locked. The look she gave him was something between pleading and demanding. His eyes filled with tears when he came to a decision.

He knew what he had to do.

"God, I'm sorry," Melvin said, his voice guttural with emotion. "Lucy... I have to take you back to the vet."

33

Melvin was sitting, waiting to see the veterinarian. It was several hours after he had let Lucy know they would have to visit the pet doctor. But he hadn't made an appointment, nor was he in the waiting area of the animal hospital.

He was sat across from it. In the back of a small, rundown coffee shop in the same plaza South Saturn Animal Hospital was located in. He was watching the door of the animal hospital, waiting for the moment Dr. Antoine Torsten stepped out and headed to his car. One of the three cars still in the parking lot of a plaza where most of the shops had closed for the night. The animal clinic had closed as well, though Melvin knew the vet liked to stay there late.

"Would you like anything else, sir?" asked the waitress, an exasperated-looking middle-aged woman with hair that surely would be greying had it not been so obviously dyed brown. The logo of the establishment on the shirt she wore was stretched by her large chest and torso, making her a walking billboard. It was a white coffee cup with steam ascending from the top and the hands of time on its side – the hour hand pointing to six, the minute hand pointing to twelve – and **Coffee O'Clock!**, the name of the chain, written boldly beneath the cup. She appeared less than thrilled with the idea of spending her night in a place like this, serving a person like him.

"Oh no, I'm fine," Melvin said, careful not to maintain eye contact with the server. He didn't want to be seen or remembered.

Melvin had ordered chicken broth and two pieces of unbuttered toast when he had sat down at the table two hours ago. He had been sipping and nibbling on the respective menu items ever since. It was all he could bring himself to consume after the violent vomiting fit he'd had that morning. He didn't want to risk another. Especially out in public where he was trying not to be noticed. Though, from the look the waitress had given Melvin after taking his original order, he may have been doing a poor job of being inconspicuous.

He was wearing a rain slicker even though there hadn't been a drop of rain all week. He had a baseball cap pulled low over his face to shade his features and cover his bloody eye. And, of course, he had a cat in a carrier on the chair beside him.

Melvin convinced himself it wouldn't matter. Neither the waitress nor the two other patrons chatting at the front of the shop knew him. They wouldn't be able to recognize or identify him if interrogated. With how haggard he looked, how worn down, he barely recognized himself. Considering what he was about to do, he realized, he no longer recognized himself on the inside either.

Yes, you do know who you are, Mel, he reminded himself. *You know you're someone who's willing to do anything to save the only creature in the world who loves you.*

He poked his finger into the side of the carrier and waggled it at Lucy. She looked at it indifferently before closing her eyes and laying her head on her paws.

They – he and Lucy – had decided that, while he couldn't go out and kill a stranger, he could justify killing the person who had caused this situation in the first place.

A sacrifice. Dr. Torsten's life for Lucy's, the cat the vet had been too greedy and heartless to attempt to save.

He sipped the cold broth from his spoon, pretended to read the newspaper on the table in front of him from time to time, and waited. He wondered – not for the first time, not for the thousandth – if this was something he should follow through with.

Melvin had done this before; the waiting, and the watching of the animal clinic from this very same seat in this very same coffee shop. That had only been two weeks ago.

He had been waiting for the veterinarian on that occasion as well. It had been after the vet had informed his snotty assistant to yet again give Melvin his options regarding Lucy's care. Those options being either an inanely expensive operation or death. And by then, the operation would have been pointless.

On that day, unwilling to go home without giving the doctor a piece of his mind, he had stayed in Coffee O'Clock for nearly two hours after the clinic had closed. When he had seen Dr. Torsten emerge from the back door of the animal hospital, Melvin had walked up and screamed at the doctor as he was attempting to get into his car, a Lincoln Continental with vanity plates that read 'PETDCTR' on them.

Melvin had shouted many incendiary terms on that night. Made a great deal of accusations. Screamed words like "murderer," like "thieving bastard." Said sentences that included profanities such as "fuck" and "prick" and "cunt."

The doctor, to his credit, had borne this all with great patience, a look of near indifference on his face that made Melvin even angrier, that stretched his rant to a tirade. When he was finally done, out of breath and out of words, the vet had simply said,

"I understand that you are going through a rough time right now, Mr. Cockburn. I appreciate your frustration. But this is not the way to go about dealing with it. I've simply told you the cost of the only procedure that may – and I once again emphasize *may* – save your cat's life. Even then, there's no guarantee of for how long. I offered you the alternative of giving your Lucy a peaceful end rather than prolonging her pain. That is all. But since you are so upset with my 'ultimatum,' as you put it, I will offer you a new one: Leave now or I'll have no choice but to report what you have been doing to the police. You have been harassing my assistant with your phone calls and your nasty words, and now this. If I didn't know and appreciate how much pain you are in, I wouldn't give you the option at all. Please try to enjoy the rest of your night."

With that, the vet had taken all of Melvin's options away by entering his car. He had started the vehicle as Melvin had stared, dumbfounded, not sure how to respond to what the vet had said. The words had shamed him, and that shame had enraged him. A paralyzing rage he had never felt before. An anesthetic of an emotion that left him feeling limp and numb.

He had watched as the doctor had begun to drive off, only to brake immediately, roll down his window, and add insult to a host of egregious injuries when he said,

"And please, do right by Lucy."

He had driven off then, leaving Melvin to stare after him and his silly licence plate. When the car was on the street and out of sight, Melvin had looked around to see if anyone had been there to witness his embarrassment. But the parking lot had been near vacant. The coffee shop was open but empty of patrons as well. There had been nobody in sight. People knew not to hang out in places like this after dark in Saturn City.

When he had noticed that absence of people – of witnesses – Melvin had a horrific thought: *I could have strangled him to death, and nobody would have known.* He had dismissed the thought. Had felt further shamed by it.

Yet here he was now, weeks later, about to turn that thought into action. Though instead of strangling the vet, his plan involved a thick plastic bag, and a knife he had sharpened for a half hour before leaving his house. At least that *had* been the plan. But now, unlike the last time he had waited here, growing angrier by the minute, Melvin was losing his resolve as the seconds ticked by.

He couldn't help but think of the woman who had exited the clinic earlier this evening, just after it had closed, a bird cage in her hand and a smile on her face. He thought of the man who had been joking with the veterinary assistant even as he left the clinic with his husky, his face an example of authentic joy as he led the dog, which had a cone over its head, to his car.

As Melvin sat there, sipping room temperature broth and gnawing on flavourless white toast, his mind was full of the images of people's pets on the animal hospital's walls; the collages of happy pet owners and their furry family members, cute little critters the veterinarian had helped or saved. It was thinking of those people, those animals, those images, that made Melvin understand that if he murdered this vet – despite him being a swindler and an asshole – he would be ridding the world of someone who saved animals and put smiles on the faces of their owners. Albeit only on the faces of those with deep pockets and large bank accounts. Still... the animals... Could he do that to them? Take away their provider of care?

He wasn't sure, but he would no longer be able to think it over. It was time for him to decide. The vet had just walked out of the clinic.

34

Melvin dropped the spoon into the bowl. It splashed and jangled in a shallow pool of cold yellow liquid, making a noise that sounded like an explosion to his tense ears. He looked up and around, worried the waitress would be there watching, practically taking notes for when the police inevitably came around asking questions about the vet Melvin was about to murder.

If he murdered him.

Melvin still wasn't sure.

The doctor was now facing the animal hospital door, locking it. Then he would take the short walk to his vehicle, and Melvin would lose his chance.

He stood. Put his hand on the handle of Lucy's carrier. Was ready to walk out of the coffee shop and do the deed he had left his house to do. But he could almost see those sick and injured animals through the walls of the clinic. Who would take care of them come morning?

Melvin couldn't do it.

He sat down, bitterly disappointed as he watched Dr. Torsten enter his car and drive off, that idiotic licence plate mocking Melvin once more.

Lucy meowed softly from the carrier. Melvin couldn't interpret the sound this time, but figured she must be upset with him.

"I'm sorry, Lucy. I just... I just couldn't. Maybe we ca–"

She meowed again, cutting him off. Peeking inside the cage, he saw that she was staring out of the coffee shop window. He turned to look at what had caught her attention, and saw a woman cutting across the parking lot.

"That fucking bitch of an assistant," he muttered as he watched the woman walk past the vet's building. It was dark out, but he would recognize her anywhere.

Before he could decide what this sighting meant for him, he heard Lucy pipe up. And this time there was no doubt what she was saying.

I'm hungry, she meowed.

More life, she reminded him.

She continued speaking to him as the woman crossed the parking lot, headed toward the sidewalk, the street. Soon she would be out of sight.

And he couldn't have that.

"Okay, Lucy," Melvin replied to her. "Okay."

Then he rose, placing a pair of two-dollar bills he had stolen from his mother's purse on the table to pay for his flavoured water and toasted bread. He collected Lucy in her carrier and left as speedily as he could while still attempting to remain inconspicuous.

35

Melvin wanted to follow her for longer than he wound up following her. Wanted to make sure he found the right spot. To ensure no one was around or would be around. But he understood that the longer he walked behind her, the greater the chances of her noticing him and running. He wouldn't be able to chase her with Lucy in his hand, and he wasn't willing to abandon his cat on the street if a pursuit became necessary.

If he had followed her for longer, she might have taken a turn into a store, walked toward a busy street, or stopped at a bus stop in full sight of motorists and passersby, few of them though there were. For these reasons, he had to cut his stalking short. Fortunately for him, they were in a part of Saturn that was over a hundred years old, with edifices closely spaced, businesses built side by side, separated by the occasional darkened alley or path, many of which contained dumpsters. There were several places around this area where a body could be grabbed and dragged to. And, so long as they kept that body silent, a person could do with it what they wished.

When he saw one of those places, an alley several yards ahead, he quickened his pace, closing the meters-long gap between he and Lucy's next meal. From the carrier, she was quiet. Lucy made no noise. Melvin knew she understood that both she and her owner were on a hunt, and stealth would be essential.

When he was a few feet behind her, he placed Lucy's carrier gently on the sidewalk. He needed both hands for what he was to do.

She was only several strides away, but it seemed as though it took a minute to close the space between them. The entire time, the night that should have been silent was thrumming, a loud and rapid drumbeat, a pounding that Melvin took some time to understand was the sound of his heart once again in his head. One heart accelerating as it closed in on another.

From his left pocket he removed a plastic grocery bag, the thickest he could find in the bag of bags his mother kept under the kitchen sink.

In three quick steps – taken while raising the bag above his head with both hands – he was directly behind her. Which is when she began to turn. Melvin nearly jumped back in surprise at her motion, the shifting of her shoulders, the pivoting of her feet. But before she could fully look behind her, before she could see what was about to happen to her, the bag descended, covering her head entirely, his closed fists hammering down on her shoulders once it did.

She gasped. He felt it as much as he heard it. He felt the bag constrict as her inward breath pulled it into her mouth and nostrils. He could imagine her surprise at the sudden blocking of every airway, each struggle for breath only cutting air off further.

He used both hands to pull the bag as taut as he could, pulling her head and body in the process. With one hand clutching the bag as though his life depended on it, because her death depended on it, he used his free arm to put this woman he so hated into a chinlock, applying pressure to her throat with his bicep and forearm.

Through the bag, against his arm, he felt her mouth moving, working to draw breath, to make noise. Her screams were trapped inside her mouth, stuck in her throat, muffled and muted there. Her feet made up for the lack of sound her mouth could produce as they stomped desperately while he dragged her by the head and neck across the paving.

She struggled. Her struggles were futile. Even in his diminished state, Melvin outweighed her by at least thirty pounds. It was nothing for him to wrench back on her head, yank her completely off those noisy feet, and drag her thrashing body into one of the many dark alleyways along this dim deserted street.

36

She was no longer thrashing, no longer grumbling and groaning from her throat. She was no longer moving other than the slow rise and fall of her chest, the only indication she was still alive.

Not wanting to waste time fumbling with the bag, Melvin left it on her head, only lifting the front of it over her lips, just enough to ensure that air could travel to her freely. He still needed her alive for the process.

He stood up from his crouched position beside the woman he had suffocated senseless, and began to run toward the mouth of the alley, looking back a time or two to make sure she was still there. To ensure she hadn't been playing possum only to spring up and dash, ruining his efforts.

At the entry of the alley, Melvin glanced out at the street to confirm that no one had seen. That no one was seeing.

What he saw was a Monday night. A poorly lit peopleless street, the society surrounding it preparing to go to sleep, most of them dreading the thought of Tuesday morning. He saw no pedestrians, no slowing or stopping motorists, no one approaching the alley to play hero. He saw no flashing lights at the top of police cruisers racing there and screeching to a halt.

He saw no witnesses.

Melvin sprinted to the cat carrier he had left on the sidewalk and retrieved Lucy. He made a painstaking effort not to run back to the alley. Instead, he walked quickly but steadily so as to not terrify his cat more than she already likely was.

Except Lucy didn't sound terrified, Melvin realized the closer he got to the unconscious body. Lucy sounded excited. Lucy sounded famished. And Melvin was determined to feed his little cat.

Upon returning to the alley, he set down the carrier and opened the door. Usually, he would be scared to let his cat out in the open air. Despite finding her outdoors, he had never treated her like an outdoor cat.

Since he had found her on that otherwise terrible day so many years ago, Lucy had only been outside when he took her for short walks on her leash. But now he was confident, felt it in his bones that his cat would not run away. Why would she? This was what she had been waiting for.

To his relief, she did not run. She walked out of the carrier, looked and sniffed at the air around her, then trotted a few steps toward the prone woman's covered head. She sat there, waiting patiently, looking at Melvin in a way that encouraged expeditiousness.

He wasn't done with the cat carrier yet. From inside of it he retrieved the knife he had used on his mother and Brian. He had wrapped it tightly with a towel and now unravelled it. Held it in his hand as he looked at the woman's barely moving chest.

He had nearly asphyxiated her to death, and might have caused brain damage due to oxygen deprivation. But none of that mattered so long as she was still alive. So long as that heart was still beating.

Looking at the chest protecting that heart, something left Melvin unsettled. He had a bad feeling as he stared at her barely rising and falling breast. A feeling he couldn't figure out. But one he didn't have time to stand there and think of. He muttered at her as he went about doing what he had to do.

"Your fault, you bitch. You could have helped us out."

Melvin unzipped her jacket.

"My last name is pronounced co-burn. *Cooooooo*-burn. Not *cock*-burn. Asshole."

He grabbed the collar of her sweater.

"Maybe if you and that fucking criminal of a vet cared enough about my Lucy, you wouldn't be here right now."

He used the knife to cut her sweater down the middle. He exposed a pink bra, which he cut open as well. He parted all material until he saw only skin.

He paused to look at that skin, at the flesh of her chest, the pale and pink of her belly. He could feel the heat of her rising and warming the cool night.

He began to cut along her sternum, the knife slicing the skin easily. As he did this, her large breasts moved, jiggling freely. As they moved, he became aroused by them, his cock having a mind of its own, deciding now was a good time to wake up and distract him. It was upon registering this arousal that Melvin began to understand what was wrong, the bad feeling he'd had while looking at her chest.

And all at once he was no longer horny.

Her tits, Melvin thought. *They're too big.*

The veterinarian's assistant was rail thin. Flat chested.

"No," Melvin whispered, stopping his cutting as small rivulets of blood began overtaking the landscape of her chest and stomach. In the darkness of this late summer night, the blood looked nearly black.

Melvin stared at the person he had made a six-inch incision in. Observed her more closely than he had before. Noticing now the difference in height. Noticing now that this unconscious woman's body was full-figured, girthy. Perceiving presently, as he looked at the bag and the hair that was poking out from under it, that she was blonde and not brunette.

"*Fuck.*" He spat the word upon realizing what he had done. He removed the bag from the veterinary assistant's head. And saw that it wasn't the veterinary assistant at all.

"But… I was sure… She looked *exactly* like her."

She did not look exactly like her now as Melvin observed this barely breathing body, this person he had attacked and smothered and dragged into an alley, this person he had half denuded before lacerating her sternum in hopes of excavating her chest. He stared unbelievingly at this woman who looked nothing at all like the veterinary assistant.

It was a mistake, it was a mistake… the words became a constant chorus in his head. But the mistake need not be made worse, Melvin understood. He had simply taken a wrong route; it wasn't too late to reverse, to turn around. She was still breathing. And he could keep her that way. He could leave her in the alley, call the paramedics from a payphone. They could stitch her up. Save her.

As if sensing the thought, Lucy, from beside this stranger's head, let loose a long, loud ululation. A siren in the silent night. It was a desperate sound Melvin had never heard before. And it frightened him, so hungry was his cat.

"I'm sorry," he said to the stranger who did not vaguely resemble the veterinary assistant he would have been pleased to murder. "But I can't stop now."

With Lucy still yowling, Melvin brought the knife back to the woman's chest.

And this time he cut her deep.

37

Melvin was walking in a daze. He had been doing so since disposing of a heartless body in a dumpster. With it was the rain slicker and hat he had worn while turning a person to a corpse. He'd thrown them in the garbage as he had done with Brian's clothes. He had also thrown up, vomiting twice since leaving the alley. Lucy had been especially eager in her eating of that stranger's heart. The sight and sounds of her feeding had sickened him.

He had decided to walk home rather than chance taking the bus. He knew that seeing anyone look at him and his cat carrier would be too much for him, too overwhelming. All of the judgmental stares he was accustomed to receiving would feel like something else. Like true judgement. The kind that comes with a courtroom, a jury, and a gavel that would punctuate a sentence Melvin wanted no part of.

Each stare could mean his incarceration, the end of life as he knew it. His separation from Lucy. He was a murderer now, truly, and every glance from a stranger was an opportunity for him to be identified by the police.

After over two hours of travelling as obscurely as he could, Melvin was nearly home. While he'd walked, he had contemplated what he had done on this night, considered carefully what his actions made him.

"It was a mistake. I didn't mean to," Melvin mumbled, as he had been doing since leaving the alley, trying to reconcile with the fact that he had killed a perfect stranger. Lucy had meowed consolations in response each time he had said those words. This time, however, he didn't hear her voice as distinctly as he had on the occasions prior. It was nearly drowned out by the music coming from a certain neighbour's house.

He heard the music even before he turned the corner that would lead to his street. He wasn't surprised to hear it, and knew exactly where it was coming from. Usually, this would be something he could ignore, but, on this night, he was in no mood for his noisy neighbours. He needed peace of mind, and their racket only served to make him peeved. The guilt over what he had done earlier was turning to anger and agitation. He might not have been so annoyed had the music been coming from any other house. But it emanated from the house belonging to the two people who bothered him even on his best day.

"Loud goddamn hippies," Melvin muttered under his breath as he neared the house which was polluting the neighbourhood with noise.

It was the house across the street from his. The place owned by the Gormans, the stay-at-home couple who spent too much time on their porch or in their backyard. Too much time drinking. The Gormans, who treated life like a never-ending party. The couple who often whispered loudly and giggled whenever he passed by. As they had when he'd last returned home from the animal hospital with his cat carrier in hand. The obnoxious music was coming from the home of the pair who made him feel unwelcome in a neighbourhood he had run around in before they had been born.

"What a fucking loser," he recalled one of them saying, both of them laughing.

And now, as he approached their house once more, the music – trance, house, some sort of electronica – seemed to be doing the laughing for them. Roaring at the neighbourhood defiantly, relishing that none of their neighbours would complain. Laughing at Melvin personally.

Well, Melvin had had enough. It was time he stood up to those two. Time for him to stop being their victim. Even if, in this case, victimhood only meant being assailed by their awful taste in music.

Lucy yipped a sound of encouragement, confirming she agreed with what he was about to do. Without giving it a second thought, Melvin turned left instead of crossing the street to go to his house. From the sidewalk, he tread the path up their walkway to their door. With the middle finger of his free hand, he pressed the doorbell. When no one answered after a few beats, he rapped upon the door. Counted down from thirty.

When he reached zero and the door remained closed and unanswered, he knocked on it harder, more loudly. Rang the bell again. Counted down from ten.

This time, when he reached zero, without thinking, he grabbed the knob. Twisted. And the door was no longer closed. Melvin turned away from the house, looking around to see if anyone was watching.

What he saw was darkened houses, closed drapes, empty sidewalk, carless street.

"I think I probably should," he responded to Lucy's meowing. With the two in agreement, Melvin walked into the house of Jill and Daniel Gorman, the neighbours across the road.

38

The electronica assaulted Melvin, blasting past him into the street. No wonder they couldn't hear the doorbell.

He had been expecting to see those two smug assholes on this level, perhaps dancing at their own private party, maybe having over a guest or two. He had intended to give them a piece of his mind, to tell them to turn down that damn racket. But there was no one here to accept his umbrage. The hallway and living room, which he could see into from the front door, were both empty. Devoid of light. Melvin hurriedly stepped inside and closed the door behind him.

Locked it.

What am I doing? he asked himself as he looked into the dark house. Dark except for the light seeping from an open doorway upstairs. He could see it from where he stood, a dim glow from the room directly across the stairs providing illumination to the otherwise lightless home. That's where the music was coming from.

He gave himself no answer before he began to walk into the house, up the stairs that were feet from the front door. Toward the bedroom, the sound of the music.

I just want to ask them to turn it down, he reasoned internally. But then, somehow, even above the sound of the roaring music, he heard Lucy meowing. And he understood that he was here to do more than reduce this couple's noise pollution.

Halfway up the stairs. All the way up. On the landing.

As Melvin crept toward the open door, he heard another sound. He could barely make it out, but it was like a slap, a clap, something colliding with skin and flesh.

Was young Mrs. Gorman in some sort of trouble? Was Mr. Gorman abusing her? Was Melvin about to walk in on a lover's quarrel turned violent? Was he really thinking about walking into that bedroom at all?

He wasn't thinking about it, he was doing it. Perhaps he was emboldened by the murder of his mother, or that of her little assistant, Brian, or maybe he was fueled by the mistake he had made earlier this night. In any case, he wasn't going to shy away. Not when he was this close.

The drumming in the music sounded more like a rapidly beating heart the closer he got to the door. He had to push it open further than it had been to fit himself and Lucy through. He did this carefully, quietly, despite knowing that even the squeakiest of hinges couldn't have been heard over the music they were playing.

What he saw in that lowly lit room nearly made him step back out of it. For a moment, he was certain that Mr. Gorman was in the midst of committing murder.

Melvin was looking at the master bedroom, specifically at the bed within it. At the two who currently occupied that bed.

Mr. Gorman had his back turned to Melvin. It was a back mostly naked. The parts of it that weren't nude were barely covered by a vest, if it could be called that. What he wore was a sparse collection of metal-studded leather straps held together by large silver hoops. On his head was a hat which resembled that of a police officer, if police attire consisted of glossy black leather. Below that mostly naked back, Melvin could see Mr. Gorman's slender but muscular bare buttocks. They were clenched as he knelt upon the bed.

Melvin looked away, feeling his face flush, feeling uncomfortable for even noticing the younger man's ass. For considering how well sculpted it was.

FELIX I.D. DIMARO

It wasn't hard for him to find something more worthy of his attention than Mr. Gorman's spectacular ass. There was the feather in the man's left hand that also caught Melvin's eye. As well as what looked like a miniature oar in his right hand. A short-handled paddle.

He was showing both objects to the person between his legs; his naked wife, who he was kneeling over. Straddling. And it was then that Melvin realized he'd walked in on something he had only seen photographed and described in the dirty magazines under his bed.

BDSM, S&M. Pain and pleasure.

Pain *or* pleasure.

Mr. Gorman was currently holding the feather and the paddle up for his wife to decide which it would be.

She never did choose. Because, as Melvin was watching in awe of the last thing he had expected to walk in on, he saw Mrs. Gorman's head peak out from the cover of her husband's body. Their eyes met. And the expression of pure anticipatory lust on her face changed into something else. Her pretty features were twisted into terror.

She began to thrash, to buck against the miniature belts around her wrists and ankles, the little straps which were attached to chains that were connected to all four ornate posts of what had to be the most lavish bed Melvin had ever seen.

In her eyes he saw a pent-up scream. One that couldn't escape her due to the vibrant pink ball gag in her mouth. She couldn't shout. Couldn't warn her husband with her words. What she did instead of yell was knock on the headboard with the backs of her chained hands as she pointed with her head, her eyes, her hips at the intruder in the room.

After several seconds, her husband finally seemed to get the hint. He turned around. But by then, Melvin had placed his cat carrier on the floor, had opened the door

138

and removed from it his knife, releasing Lucy in the process.

The eyes of the two men met. One set confused, one set crazed.

"What are you…" Because of the music, Melvin didn't hear the words Mr. Gorman spoke even as he interrupted them by charging at the married man, knife first, the pointed part aimed at his neighbour's gut. He had instead read the beginning of the question on Mr. Gorman's lips.

Only inches from him now, Melvin was still watching those lips as they took the shape of an 'o'. An expression of surprise. Then they changed shape again into a contorted grimace.

The paddle fell, the feather floated to the bed.

Their eyes reconnected, now sharing the same understanding. One set dismayed by it, the other set delighted. Both sets of eyes displayed an awareness that this moment they were entwined in was murder.

Melvin could feel the blood pouring on the hand he had curled around the handle of his knife. The knife which was buried in the midsection of Mr. Gorman to the hilt, his stomach taking in every one of the eight inches of the blade. Their eyes still connected, Melvin saw that the life was fleeing from his neighbour.

"Not yet," he whispered. "You can't die yet."

Then, knowing that time was of the essence, he lay Mr. Gorman's dying body atop of that of his writhing, crying, still-gagged wife.

Melvin removed the knife from the younger man's stomach. Brought it to his chest.

And began to quickly but carefully carve.

39

All three of them, as well as the bed, a great deal of the wall behind the bed, and much of the carpet, were red by the time Melvin had finished cutting Daniel Gorman from sternum to stomach, removed his beating heart and set it on the floor in front of Lucy.

Exhausted from his efforts both here and in the alley, not to mention the long walk to this place, Melvin slumped on top of the body he had butchered. He watched with equal parts revulsion and elation as Lucy ate, appearing to grow stronger, more vigorous with each swallowed bit of heart.

So pleased was Melvin that he nearly forgot there was a living breathing body beneath the dead one he was leaning against as he watched his cat feast. His attention only turned back to Jill Gorman when he felt movement beneath him, heard her gag-stifled screams.

Sighing, growing wearier simply from the thought of the task ahead, Melvin turned to his cat, who had entirely consumed the heart of Mr. Gorman. It was now scraps of vein and membrane in a puddle of blood on the carpet.

"You still hungry, Lucy?"

Looking up, her whiskers red, her teeth coated in blood and pieces of an organ meant to keep a body living, the cat meowed in response. An affirmation.

Willing his weakened body to task, Melvin rose, grabbed Mr. Gorman's freshly made corpse by the ankles and yanked him from atop his wife. He pulled him all the way from the bed, allowing his body to crumple, to fold upon itself like the bundled blanket it landed beside on the floor – a comforter which had likely been thrown off the bed during this couple's bizarre night of sex.

Melvin then turned his attention to the newly made widow laying completely naked on the bed. And though he told himself he wasn't a bad guy, told himself that this was a necessity, a life for a life, he relished how her eyes bulged, how her nostrils doubled in size. He enjoyed seeing her head thrash back and forth upon her craning neck, turning first to Mr. Gorman's corpse then back to Melvin, the intruder in her house, the murderer of her husband. The man who was now crawling on the bed toward her.

He was crawling between her naked legs. Legs which were splayed open by her shackles, everything between them exposed. Every wrinkle, every fold, every razor-bumped bit of her.

He could smell her. Salty sweet. A dish he wanted to savour. And he couldn't help but inhale deeply so he could smell her more.

It had been so long.

Now, moving less comfortably than he had moments before, his erection tangled in his pants, Melvin continued to crawl up her body. He placed his left leg over her thigh, the knee coming down beside her right hip. He did the same on her opposite side. He straddled her as her husband had, looking down at her with Mr. Gorman's blood all over his hands, his clothes, spattered on his face. Melvin could feel it there – on his cheeks, on his forehead, and his lips – wet and hot. He licked his lips involuntarily. The blood on his tongue tasted like a penny smells.

He had something to say, but the music pounded obnoxiously around them. He told himself that was why he leaned against her, pressed his body onto hers. Told himself he lay atop her so she could better hear him. But the truth was he wanted her to feel him. He wanted to feel her too.

He placed his crimson coated face against hers, put his mouth to her ear. With her husband's blood painting her cheek red, Melvin said,

"I ain't so funny now, am I?"

She tried to scream then, really and truly scream directly into his ear, or perhaps past it, to the outside world for help. But even if the gag hadn't prevented the sound from leaving the house, the music would have. The electronic noise would have swallowed it.

Understanding that her attempts at shouting were useless, she tried to smash the side of her head against his, attempting to knock him out, to knock him off her. But the motions felt more like a series of nudges given her positioning and his close proximity to her.

Next, she tried to buck him off of her, pushing up on him with her midsection, thrusting her pelvis into his crotch. But when she recognized that he was enjoying this action, her stomach grinding against his hardness, she put her movement to an end. All except for an involuntary trembling as she wept with her whole body.

He realized then, with a swelling sense of sadness, that this was the most intimate moment he'd ever had with anyone. He only raised himself from her when he felt the tears quake through her; looking down at her face, he saw what he feared he would see.

Repulsion, revulsion. He recognized those feelings in her face. Recognized them because he had so often seen them on the face of his mother for a variety of reasons.

Did she think I was going to rape her? he wondered, horrified. Then, adding to that horror, he asked himself other questions:

Were you going to rape her?

Isn't what you've done so far rape enough already?

He didn't ponder the questions for long because the look on her face had brought with it the thought of his mother. And the thought of his mother made the matter moot. His erection was dwindling. He was glad for that.

142

This wasn't about violation. This was a sacrifice to save a life.

He wasn't a monster, after all.

With his upper body no longer pressed against her naked torso, she began to thrash and fight once more, banging her knuckles against the headboard, alternating that with attempts to pull her hands and legs free of their shackles. Unfortunately for Mrs. Gorman, her husband had done too fine a job of securing her there.

Melvin looked at her face, saw her layers of makeup smeared by blood, snot and tears. He focused on the gag in her mouth, a pink ball surrounded by painted pink lips. He heard her desperate moans and screams against it, and that's when he considered something he hadn't before: How could she have used her safe word gagged like that? Would she maybe snap her fingers if things got too intense with the feather or the paddle? Would she groan in a certain way that would get her now dead husband to hold back?

It was then he took note of her repeated knocking of the headboard behind her. Was that the safe signal? A particular rapping on the wood? Was she hoping it might work even now? That, by some miracle, he would understand the signal and stop what he was determined to do?

There was a jolting absence of noise as one song stopped and another began. In the gap of silence, Melvin heard Lucy meowing from the floor, imploring him to fetch her a third meal for the night.

"One second, Lucy," he said over his shoulder just as the music began to pound again.

He had placed the knife on the bed beside Mrs. Gorman as he'd crawled over her body. Now he retrieved it, and watched whatever revulsion had been on her face be overtaken by undressed dread.

"You'll be with your husband again soon!" he shouted down to her over the synthetic sounds playing from their stereo speaker as he raised the knife. Like a man riding a saddleless horse, he had to press his thighs against her sides to stabilize himself as she attempted to fight him off.

He brought the tip of the knife down to the center of her heaving chest. Watched it part her skin, sink into her flesh. He saw the blood begin to pool before running down her stomach, first a single rivulet leading from the wound to the hollow of her belly button, filling it, then more blood spilling beneath both breasts, down her ribs, dripping onto the sheets.

She stopped thrashing. He felt her stilling beneath him. Perhaps she was worried that her movements might make things worse, might cause her to die faster. That was his concern. The extraction of the heart was always an arduous affair.

The bloody cut he created between her chest and stomach was several inches long. By the time he stopped sawing, by the time he removed the knife from her, she was barely moving. He could see her stomach and chest rising, knew she was alive. He could practically hear her heart beating along to the music that was playing from the speakers.

And now was the tricky part.

Melvin went to push inside of her. To place his hand inside the opening in her chest. But that's when Lucy appeared in front of him. She climbed partially on top of Mrs. Gorman, her back paws on the bed, her front paws on the dying woman's stomach. Lucy looked longingly into the cavity Melvin had created. She then looked up at her owner, her friend, the only family she had known over these last dozen years, and purred softly. That was enough for him to understand.

"You want to get it yourself?" he asked her. She meowed, moved her head in a gesture that seemed, to Melvin, exactly like a human nod.

"Hurry up then," he said, not unkindly. He stayed sitting on the body in case Mrs. Gorman woke up and began to buck again. He didn't want her efforts at survival to interfere with Lucy's feeding.

Lucy crept fully onto the woman's stomach, her paws on either side of the open wound. The cat sniffed once, licked at the blood still pumping from the injury, then she pressed her nose into the opening. She forced the flesh to part further as she pushed her mouth, her head, into Mrs. Gorman's chest.

It took some effort, Melvin observed. Lucy's muscles bunched up in her legs as her claws dug into Mrs. Gorman's bloodied stomach while she worked her way inside the widow. Gaining traction, she forced herself deeper into the wound.

Once she was inside of the young woman up to her middle – only her hindquarters and tail showing – Lucy must have found the heart, because that was when Mrs. Gorman came back to consciousness.

Her eyes opened, her body reared up. Melvin barely avoided being thrown off. He held on and watched Lucy do the same, plunging her rear claws deeper into the taut skin of Mrs. Gorman's stomach.

The cat continued to eat her way into the young woman's body, continued to tear and rend her heart. The entire time, the muffled screams of Lucy's living meal were drowned out by the sounds of electronica.

40

Mrs. Gorman had been still for minutes, her eyes open and staring lifelessly at the ceiling by the time Lucy backed herself out of the woman's cooling corpse. The cat was mostly red after she had done so. From her nose to her back legs, she was wet, her fur and onesie thickly matted with blood, ornamented here and there with pieces of viscera and flesh.

Lucy climbed down from the body and sat on the mattress. She licked around her mouth furiously, as if attempting to savour every morsel of her last meal. Fruitlessly, she attempted to groom herself, to lick her body clean of the blood which overwhelmed it.

"Oh, Lucy! look at the mess you've made!" Melvin said, smiling as he spoke, his voice full of affection. He looked down at himself and saw that he was just as much a mess. "Shower time it is!" he told his cat, nearly singing out the words.

He removed himself from the dead body and stood beside the bed as he stripped himself of his clothes. Once he was naked, Melvin stopped to observe what he had done to the married couple. He glanced at the husband, looked to the wife. And continued to look at her. At her breasts, reddened, sitting oddly placed on her open chest, but still somehow enticing. He looked below the bloodbath of her upper body at her cleaner lower half. Stared between her legs.

He considered something awful just then. It had been *so* long, and he had only been with women he had paid for. But this would be different.

This would be tender. This would be intimate.

"No," he told himself. And listened to himself, too.

Melvin collected his cat and walked to the bathroom adjoining the master bedroom. For a moment he considered taking Lucy into the shower with him, but remembered the bites, scratches, and gouges she had given him when he had tried to bathe her shortly after finding her all those years ago. He didn't want to add his blood to all that had already spilled inside this house. He decided on wetting a towel and wiping Lucy down as best he could before leaving her on the bathroom mat and walking into the shower. There, she could lick herself clean to her satisfaction.

He stayed in the shower just long enough to feel unsoiled, relishing the soap and water on his skin, washing as he watched the bottom of the tub turn from dark red to sudsy pink to full of white bubbles and clear water. The synthetic music played the entire while.

As he cleaned, Melvin noticed that his head was nodding, his shoulders were bopping and twitching, his hips rocking almost imperceptibly.

Maybe this music ain't so bad, he thought, smiling as he swayed inside the shower.

41

Melvin, with Lucy in his arms, made it all the way into the bedroom from the bathroom before he had to head right back.

Upon seeing the bodies, the blood, he placed Lucy on the bed, turned, and ran directly to the toilet. There, he released the contents of his stomach. He found he needed to throw up each time Lucy fed. In the moment, he could handle it; he could maintain his composure while watching her. But something about the aftermath seemed to trigger his system, make him spew. And this scene was somehow worsened because of how clean he currently was. Clean and naked. A contradiction to the crimson-coloured chaos around him.

He was too clean for the clothes he had worn there. They, like everything in the bedroom, were now red. Drenched. After flushing the toilet and stopping at the sink to rinse out his mouth, Melvin went back to the Gormans' bedroom.

The music had finally stopped. The room, the house, was silent.

At first, he tried to avoid setting his eyes on the mess he'd made, but the mess he'd made was everywhere, unignorable. Looking at the walls, the sheets, the carpet, the bed, the word 'massacre' came to Melvin's mind. The words 'blood bath.'

Entrails, insides, hung out of the open midsections of both Gormans. Melvin felt his stomach churn, but he didn't need to vacate it again. With his mind and body adjusting, getting used to being surrounded by a murder scene, he walked into the room and headed for the closet opposite the foot of the bed.

He couldn't avoid stepping into blood. The carpet had soaked up all that had flowed out of Mr. Gorman, as the mattress was absorbing the blood of his wife.

He opened the closet door and was surprised to see how dark it was. Fumbling his hand against the interior wall until he found a switch, Melvin turned on the light and found himself looking at a closet that was a little room; something he could walk into, which was what he did.

It was nothing like the little clothes rack he'd had in the corner of his laundry room since he was fourteen years old, from which hung his handful of outfit choices – four button down shirts, three of which he hadn't worn in a decade, two pairs of jeans, a pair of slacks, a pair of chinos. This was like walking into a clothing store.

On the right hung Mr. Gorman's clothes, to Melvin's left hung Mrs. Gorman's. Among their plethora of stylish garments, Melvin could see a collection of racy costumes. Items like the outfit Mr. Gorman had died in on this night.

There were leather vests, a variety of masks, latex dresses so small they looked to be sized for a large doll rather than an adult woman. There was what looked to be a mascot uniform hanging in the closet, some animal Melvin couldn't easily identify. Perhaps it was a cat.

Dangling from a standing rack at the back of the closet was an array of what looked like weaponry: whips, chains, a longer more ornate paddle than the one Mr. Gorman had been about to use on his wife when Melvin had stabbed him in the belly. Near it was a black feather duster with a handle that was shaped like the longest and thickest cock Melvin had ever seen. There was a belted strap-on, the phallus portion neon pink. Another strap-on, the pretend penis replete with painful looking silver studs.

Below the hanging clothes and around the rack of pain and pleasure, were rack after rack of shoes.

Sneakers, loafers, heels, flats, more shoes than any two reasonable people should have owned.

"Goddamn hippie freaks," Melvin whispered.

He looked upon it all with a bitter taste in his mouth that had nothing to do with what he had vomited. The taste in his mouth was jealousy. He was envious of two corpses. They'd had so much, they'd had each other. While he'd had nothing but his mother's basement, his mother's scorn. No friends, no lovers, no love. What he'd had was the Gormans' laughter and mockery.

You at least have the last laugh, he reminded himself. And, as he had done after killing Brian, he laughed aloud as if to prove this true. A trilling titter. Nervous noise.

In addition to the last laugh, he now also had his choice of several outfits. He picked a pair of fancy blue jeans, stepped into them. He grabbed a white, collared shirt he could never have afforded, and put that on, tucking the shirt into the jeans. The clothes were too large for him, but that wasn't a concern. He found a brown belt and brown loafers before leaving the closet.

He was too excited by this change of clothes to much care about the blood or bodies he was surrounded by back in the room. Melvin wanted to see himself in the mirror.

You could use a haircut, and your eye is still a mess, but not bad. Not bad at all. He smiled at his reflection in the mirror on the fancy dresser by the bed. He felt confident. He felt like a somebody. He felt as if he had become the man he had just gutted, whose heart he had extracted and fed to his cat.

"How do I look, honey?" he said, turning from the grand bureau mirror to the bed. He spoke in his best impersonation of Mr. Gorman (which wasn't very good at all), making his voice nasally and high pitched. It was a closer imitation of a talking rat than of the man he had slain. "Think I look sexy?"

He strutted beside the dresser a few paces, his strides like those of a runway model. When he got to the edge of the mirror he turned dramatically, went back up the runway, spun and posed for the body on the bed.

"Does this make you *waaaaant* me?" he asked lustily, then released a short, frantic laugh before immediately growing serious. His face now solemn, sullen, he said, "God, you're beautiful, hon." Then he stepped closer to the bed.

Her face was smeared and freckled with red, her neck was entirely that colour. Her breasts were too far apart as a result of the hole he had made in her chest and stomach. A hole Lucy had somehow extended until it was the size of Melvin's head. But aside from that, she was nearly perfect. In places that weren't entirely covered in blood, he could see the milky white skin of her legs. And he could see between them once again.

Somehow, above the scent of leaked life that overwhelmed the room, above the smell of Mr. Gorman's posthumous bowel movement, he could smell her salty sweetness.

He stepped toward the bed until there were no more steps to take, placed a hand on a dry portion of her thigh. It was cool, it was soft.

This could still be tender, he thought again.

This could still be intimate.

Beside Mrs. Gorman's body was Lucy. She had been grooming herself, but now, as Melvin contemplated what he would do, the baggy pants he wore feeling less baggy, the cat watched him as if waiting to see how this would go.

"No," Melvin said once more, removing his hand from Mrs. Gorman's thigh. He watched, fascinated, as he saw the imprint of his fingers dimpling her flesh, then vanishing as though she had never been touched at all.

"That's not who I am. Time for us to go, Lucy."

He gathered his cat and his bloody attire, put them all in the carrier. Then, wearing both clothing and a sense of confidence unfamiliar to him, Melvin exited the Gormans' house and walked home carrying a healthy cat, a smile on his face as he strode across the street.

42

Melvin was sitting in his mother's favourite spot on the sofa the next morning. Lucy was on his lap. He was weeping. He was holding her close and crying into her fur. Fur which had no silly onesie covering it.

He had come home the previous night after murdering one stranger and two neighbours, and had fallen asleep wearing one of those neighbours' clothes after once again being violently ill. Lacking the strength to crawl up the stairs to his mother's room, or to descend the stairs to his own, he had stumbled to the living room and fallen asleep in his mother's favourite seat.

When he had woken up in the morning, he noticed that the television was playing, though he couldn't recall having turned it on after coming home. It was on a station he never watched. A station which was currently broadcasting the morning news. But he paid no mind to the TV, his attention had been all for his cat.

Lucy had been on the opposite end of the couch, tugging and chewing at a onesie that had only been wiped with a wet towel while they were at the Gormans' house and was now stained red and pink. He hadn't had the energy to change her upon their return the night before, and the material of the little outfit had stiffened overnight, irritating the cat. Lucy had been worrying at it, trying to remove it from her body.

She had hated the covering from the start. Even before the tumour had become truly horrendous, the onesie alone had stifled Lucy's movements, making her less than what she had been.

He remembered putting it on her for the first time, watching her walk in a circle and then dramatically fall to her side immediately after. Looking up at him, her expression had been a plea for him to remove what he had forced her to be constrained in. It had been heartrending.

From that point on, she had stopped jumping unless absolutely necessary, had stopped running around. It was as though the garment had been her own personal cage, keeping her imprisoned no matter where she moved.

"Sorry, girl," Melvin had said upon waking this morning and noticing Lucy's agitated state. Then he had gone to get a change of onesie, new pads. Had gently removed Lucy's little article of protective clothing. And what he had seen upon doing so had reduced him to weeping.

"Holy shit..." Melvin had said, a whisper full of awe.

In the background, the television continued to drone on, to be ignored. To Melvin, the entire world may as well have fallen away. Everything else had ceased to matter. Because Lucy's lump – that wretched, life-sucking tumour – had closed up entirely.

It had shrunk as well. Had returned to being the small, pink bump it had been when Melvin had convinced himself for weeks that it was nothing but an irritation that would eventually heal on its own. Finally, it seemed as though it was doing so. Melvin could see orange and white hairs already growing out of the pink mass. He knew, without a doubt, that Lucy could be healed. He knew as well that there was nothing that would stop him until he made her whole again.

He now sat with a naked Lucy on the couch, no longer needing that obnoxious, constrictive garment that had bothered her so. He was crying onto her, hugging her until she squirmed to be let go.

"We'll be okay, Lucy. We'll be okay," Melvin whispered repeatedly while stopping her from leaping off his lap. The television, however, offered a potential contradiction to his promise.

From the news reporter came words that Melvin heard as nothing but background noise. Some sentences made their way to his hearing, but none of them fully registered despite these being words he should have been paying close attention to.

"...Some disturbing breaking news... this next story is of a grisly nature... The police have identified the woman found murdered and mutilated inside of a garbage collection bin... Melanie Thompson... Saturn City's latest homicide victim... a single mother... body was found by a store owner... The strangest and most disturbing detail... the killer had removed and taken Ms. Thompson's heart... warning citizens to stay vigilant... If you have any information, please call Crime Stoppers..."

Melvin continued hugging his cat and crying tears of joy.

43

Melvin couldn't ignore the news all day, though he did his best to.

After Lucy had finally managed to pull herself free of his bearhug of an embrace, he had delighted in seeing how quickly she had dashed away. Lightning fast, just as she had always been before she had gotten sick. He didn't mind her running from him, he knew she would be back.

And she was back. Minutes later, after tiring herself out by scrambling around the house, she came and hopped up on her owner's lap, turning in circles, making herself comfortable before laying there. He put his hand on her uncovered back, relishing the feeling of his fingers in her fur.

"Welcome back, Luce."

And the two sat on the recliner while Melvin watched daytime television: Maury Povitch, The Price is Right, The Young and the Restless, everything but the news. It was only when he saw an advertisement for that night's Toronto Blue Jays game, which he had somehow forgotten about during all the recent chaos, that he decided to go to the front door and get the day's newspaper.

His mother subscribed to the Saturn Sun, the more salacious of the news outlets in their town. When she had finished reading through the day's worth of crime and scandal, she would toss the paper down to Melvin. He didn't read the articles but he could identify the headlines. More importantly, he could check scores all around each sports league, which was what he now intended to do. He wanted to catch up on the hockey leagues, the National Basketball Association, Major

League Baseball; he wanted to find out how the race for the Grey Cup was going in the Canadian Football League. He needed something normal to get his mind off the fact that he had murdered enough people within a week to qualify as a serial killer. It wasn't a label he had ever wanted. But, as he smiled down at Lucy stretching on the floor after he had gently removed her from his lap, he understood that the label was worth it if it meant his best friend was better.

He only second guessed that notion when he opened the front door and picked the paper up from the stoop, his heart jolting as he pieced together what was written bold and black across the front page.

Would what he had done be worth it if he got caught? he wondered as he looked at the headline.

SINGLE MOTHER HORRIFICALLY SLAIN IN THE STREETS OF SATURN

The headline was easy enough for him to read despite his dyslexia. The picture of the police tape around the dumpster he had heaved a woman's body into the night before was indication enough of what the front-page article was about, even if he wasn't able to read it.

"It doesn't matter," he whispered to himself. "You were careful."

He looked up at the house across the street from his. He could see the Gormans' place clearly. It appeared serene, peaceful. It made him shudder.

How long will it be before they discover the mess I left over there? Melvin wondered as he returned inside his home with the newspaper in his hand.

44

Seven hours was the answer to the question Melvin had asked himself as he returned inside with the newspaper that morning. The first of those seven hours was as stressful as any time he could remember.

Upon going to the kitchen table and opening the newspaper to check the sports section, he was met by another surprise. It was a picture of a young man he recognized. The young man he had murdered days ago. On the page, along with the photo, were the words:

MISSING: FORMER CAPTAIN OF THE SATURN SHINING STAR, BRIAN NORTON

Melvin fought the frustration that always came with reading. Struggling to reorder the letters in his mind, guessing at familiar looking words to make the task tolerable, he was able to garner that the police had found Brian's car at the mall and there was now a small reward for any information that would lead to the missing athlete's whereabouts. Melvin had been sick again after processing what was in the paper, and what it might mean for him.

He had spent the rest of those seven hours immersed in other worlds than this one, getting lost in his television with Lucy on his lap.

Now, minutes after watching an exciting but heartbreaking loss by the Blue Jays to the Boston Red Sox, Melvin was flipping through the channels, searching for what he would watch next, when, to his amazement, on the television, he saw his own house.

He jumped in his seat, his surprise at viewing his house on the TV was so great. Lucy leapt from his lap, landed on the carpet, and looked back at him with an expression of annoyance.

He didn't bother to apologize to her as he usually would. He was too fixated by his house on the television screen, and the fact that there were police cars all along his block. He was frozen where he sat, though his head, his heart, and his body were burning with fear as it occurred to him that this could truly be the end. Of his freedom, of any time he had left with Lucy. The end of his life as he knew it.

Was Melvin about to be on an episode of *Cops*? Were they going to record live his violent arrest?

Forehead sweaty, heart pounding, he looked from his television to the direction of his front door several times in the space of a few seconds, expecting to see the police rushing toward the door on the TV, anticipating them crashing through it and coming running down the hallway in his house.

But the police did not break down his door. After fighting off his initial panic, he could see that the cops on his screen weren't paying attention to his house at all. And soon neither was the cameraman. The camera panned to the right, eventually focusing on two women standing on the sidewalk.

One of them was Mrs. Chloe Thames, widow and habitual survivor. A tall blonde woman stood beside Mrs. Thames with a microphone in her hand. It was then Melvin noticed the City Pulse logo on the corner of his screen. It matched that which was on the woman's mic. He was watching a live news report, and Mrs. Thames was being interviewed. This, he could not ignore.

"I mean... I'm just shocked," Mrs. Thames said from the TV, her face indicating that she was telling the truth. She looked from the camera to an area across the street, where Melvin could hear voices, movement, commotion. An investigation. He now understood what was going on. The police had somehow discovered the bodies of the Gormans. His street was now a crime scene. And the cops were on the hunt for the worst type of criminal.

Him.

Mrs. Thames looked more worn down than she had when he'd returned Obi to her days ago. The news of her neighbours' deaths had obviously shaken her badly.

"This is such a peaceful and quiet street. I can't believe something like this could have happened here."

Melvin scoffed at that, thinking of all the times the Gormans had disrupted the street with their music and their mocking mirth. With loud barbeques and gatherings he was never invited to. Theirs wasn't the quiet and peaceful street Mrs. Thames believed it to be. Not for Melvin Cockburn.

"They were nice people," she continued. Melvin rolled his eyes. "They were always outdoors, barbequing and enjoying the weather when it was good. Sometimes even when it wasn't. They were the life of this street. It's hard to believe something like this could happen. Especially after what was done to that poor woman this morning." She shook her head, looked into the camera as if speaking directly to Melvin. "It's hard to feel safe in this town anymore."

The camera then panned from Mrs. Thames to the scene across the street from her. The Gormans' house was surrounded by yellow tape. Uniformed officers and plainclothes police roamed the area. There was an ambulance and several squad cars parked along the curb. A fire truck, looking like a misplaced behemoth, was also in the road.

One woman was in the center of it all. On her knees, on the sidewalk, wailing inconsolably as several of the first responders tended to her, attempting to guide her from the scene.

Melvin dashed from his chair to the front door. He sat on the entryway bench that was beside it. The bench was a functional piece of furniture Moira Cockburn had purchased when she had realized she could no longer simply bend and put on her shoes. That damn hip of hers.

After purchasing the bench, she had developed the strange habit of sitting on it and staring out the window beside their front door, watching the neighbourhood for hours at a time. Melvin did now as his mother had done so often; he parted the blinds and looked out the window at the scene across the street that had just been on his TV. The entire experience was disorienting.

"Whoa!" he cried out, shocked momentarily. He was startled not by what was going on outside but by Lucy leaping onto his lap. He still wasn't quite used to her being so energetic. "You almost gave me a heart attack, girl," he whispered to her, his voice low as though he worried the police might hear him speaking through the door from all the way across the street and realize what he had done.

He positioned Lucy so she could see out of the window as well. He stroked her head as they both stared out at the street, watching police officers and reporters, onlookers and family members milling about the house. Those authorized to do so were going in and out of it. Those not authorized to enter the dwelling were approaching the authorities with what – based on their body language – appeared to be questions. Many of them.

Melvin watched a man move toward a police officer, his arms flailing as he spoke, his body trembling as he listened. Melvin imagined that all the questions being asked, everything being discussed, boiled down to one concern: finding out who did this.

"You see all those people out there, Lucy?" Melvin whispered to his cat, his chin resting on the back of her head, his lips grazing the top of it as he spoke. "All of those police officers out there, this whole entire city… Everybody is looking for us."

45

The sound of a loud thump, which seemed to come from directly beside his head, woke Melvin from his sleep. He was confused as he came to consciousness, noting that he was sitting and not laying down. That he wasn't in his or any bed.

He expected to be in his basement, in his recliner, the place he most often fell asleep sitting. But when he opened his eyes he saw that he was on his mother's bench in the foyer. And the sound he'd heard had been something banging against the front door.

Melvin's heart responded to this with a banging of its own. But while the noise against his door had been a single thud, his heart was repeatedly crashing against his chest. He wondered if it could be the police there, ready to smash through the door, to take him out of it, into their car. To lock him away forever. But wouldn't they have announced themselves by now?

He stopped wondering and questioning and decided to find out. Carefully, not wanting whoever might be at his door to see him through the blinds, he parted them and looked out into the street. Looked out at a world on the cusp of day, sitting innocently beneath a prettily painted pink and yellow sky.

He didn't see a police car on his driveway or on the street by the curb. What he did see was a young boy, perhaps twelve years old judging by his size. The boy was walking rapidly away from Melvin's door.

Some sort of prank, he thought. Or was it a message this boy was delivering from somebody who had witnessed Melvin murder his neighbours? Would he look outside and see a brick on his mother's doormat with a note elastic-banded to it? On that note, an eerily scrawled message stating: I know what you did. A warning, some request of ransom from someone who could use what he had done against him.

"You've been watching too many of them goddamn soaps," Melvin said to himself. And was mildly surprised to find that he had said the words in his mother's voice. The voice he would use to mock her when he was certain she couldn't hear him. To his ears, just then, it sounded too close to the real thing for comfort.

Without thinking more of it, he opened the door and called out to the boy who was now on the street, about to walk out of Melvin's field of vision.

"Hey! What do you think you're doing, kid?"

The boy jumped at the harsh voice breaking the quiet of an otherwise tranquil morning. He turned, seemed about to answer, but then only stopped and stared, looking at Melvin's body with an expression of confusion on his face.

Melvin followed the boy's eyes, looked down at himself, and saw that he was wearing his mother's pale peach robe. Below that, his legs were bare, and shaved of their usual coating of coarse hair. His feet were dressed in his mother's ridiculous plush cow slippers.

When did I do all this? he asked himself, astonished. And became concerned when he realized he had no answer. He only remembered sitting and staring out of his house at the police and the neighbours, some of whom he could still see now milling around the Gormans' home. Though there were nowhere near as many authorities and onlookers on the property as there had been the night before.

"I said: what are you doing throwing stuff against my house, kid?" Melvin called out hastily, the conviction gone from his voice as embarrassment began to cloud his mind. He wanted the boy to answer and leave. To stop staring at his robe and legs and slippers. This wasn't exactly the best time to draw attention to himself.

"I was just delivering your paper, sir?... Ma'am? Geeze!" said the afroed preteen as he turned and continued along the road. Melvin saw that he was rolling a cart full of newspapers behind him.

How did I miss that? he wondered, looking from the cart back to his porch, where he saw a rolled-up newspaper beside his right foot. *And that...*

He bent over to pick up the paper.

"Ms. Cockburn? How are you? I'm sorry about Obi getting into your yard the other d– Oh! I'm sorry, Melvin. I thought you were your mother!"

Melvin felt his face grow hot before he raised his head to meet the eyes of Mrs. Thames. She was standing at the bottom of the path leading to his front door, Obi was on a leash beside her. The expression on her face suggested she felt nearly as embarrassed as he did. Though there was a hint of amusement there, too.

Is she laughing at me? The idea of his only good neighbour mocking him was a thundercloud in his mind.

Deciding it would be best to make light of the situation, Melvin attempted to let out laughter of his own. But the noise he made sounded more like a poor actor's imitation.

"Hey, Mrs. Thames. Hey, Obi! Glad to see you out of that walking boot, Mrs. Thames! Felt like you were in that thing forever!" He was genuinely happy for her.

"Thank you... My doctor says I have to take it easy or else I might reinjure it. But I'm just glad I can properly walk Obi again. Even if it's just a little bit at a time for now." She was speaking but she seemed distracted, taking not so discreet glances at Melvin's attire. Still blushing, he looked down before looking back at Mrs. Thames.

"My only robe is in the wash, so I borrowed one of my mom's," he said, damning himself internally for not being able to avoid sounding like he was telling a complete lie. "It's cold as the dickens in there," he added, gesturing to his house.

As the dickens? Melvin thought, feeling foolish for saying it. *What does that even mean?*

But it didn't matter, Mrs. Thames appeared to believe the lie. She seemed less embarrassed for him, less like she was ready to dash away.

"It's chilly over at my place, too... Did you catch a cold, Melvin? You don't look so well," she inquired gently. He might have thought the comment rude if there wasn't so much concern behind it. He wasn't sure what he looked like this morning, but he didn't feel so well. Hadn't felt well in days.

In the bathroom of the Gormans', he had thought the vomiting was because he couldn't stand the scene he had left in the bedroom. He had thought the same in the alley with the stranger he had killed. And in the kitchen with his mom and Brian.

But it must have been something else.

Maybe his nerves were acting up, causing this reaction. He had left two murder scenes for the authorities. And now it was only a matter of time before the police investigating the Gormans' house would start canvassing the area, looking for a suspect. That was enough to make anyone sick.

"Just a little stomach issue, I think. Thanks for asking," he responded wanly, looking over Mrs. Thames's head, watching the few remaining police officers and detectives go in and out of the Gorman house, a group of them talking on the lawn. His stomach upset him at the thought of the police searching for a killer, piecing together clues that would result with him as the completed puzzle.

"Have you not heard what happened there?" a surprised sounding Mrs. Thames inquired. His curiosity over what was going on across the street was obvious enough for her to feel inclined to ask.

Melvin wasn't sure how to answer. He simply shook his head. Said nothing.

"Oh... God, it's so hard to even think about..." She took a deep breath, and Melvin could see that the woman was still upset by what had happened across the street. Injured by it. It nearly made him feel bad for what he had done. He hadn't meant to hurt Mrs. Thames' feelings.

"Jill and Daniel Gorman were murdered maybe... two nights ago? It's hard to say. The police found their bodies yesterday after her mother came by to visit. She is *devastated*. Jill was her only child."

Melvin recalled the woman from last night. The one in hysterics in front of the Gormans' house. He had killed someone's only child on the same night he had killed someone else's single mother. He hadn't thought about it that way before. About all the sad people he was making. He didn't like the way it felt when he thought about it now.

"What kind of sick fuck would do something like this?" Mrs. Thames asked bitterly.

This sick fuck, Melvin thought morosely. *Literally.*

"My stomach. It's acting up again. Hearing that didn't help," Melvin said meekly.

"Oh no! I'm sorry, Melvin! Is there anything I can do?"

"No, no. I'll be fine. No need to be sorry. It's not your fault. Thanks for letting me know what happened, Mrs. Thames. Bye, Obi!"

He saw both owner and dog tilt their heads and look at him with near identical quizzical expressions.

Not giving Mrs. Thames a chance to reply, he retreated into his house, closing the door behind him. He had to see what was written in the paper.

Melvin was angry at himself for opening the door dressed as his mother. He was also worried about not being able to remember when he had put her clothing on. Or why. He regretted having the paperboy and Mrs. Thames see him the way he was, dressed strangely, unprepared for even a little human interaction. He knew he had to keep a low profile, not behave suspiciously, because, after unrolling the newspaper, it was made clear to him that suspicious behaviour was what everyone in this city would now be looking for.

"Goddamnit!" Melvin said, irritated as he struggled for minutes to piece together a great deal of that morning's newspaper. The front page, several other articles, all of it was about him. And each piece referred to him and what he had done with the same few words, making his job of understanding the paper slightly easier.

They repeatedly used the word 'murder.'

The word 'serial.'

The word 'killer.'

The headline of the paper in his hands read:

A SERIAL MURDERER IN SATURN CITY: WHAT THE POLICE KNOW ABOUT THE 'AZTEC KILLER'

46

Melvin had felt poorly before looking at the newspaper. Reading it had made him feel worse. Bodily. Mentally.

He was officially a wanted man. The idea of it was so foreign, so previously inconceivable, that he was almost disconnected from it. The police were looking for him, calling him a murderer – a serial killer. He had even been given one of those creepy nicknames they all received once they were inevitably made into news sensations. The Aztec Killer. *He* was a news sensation!

Melvin felt like he was in a nightmare with his eyes open. One where he could move but could not avoid what might befall him, even when he could see devastation straight ahead. It was too much for his mind to properly process. Too much for his stomach as well. He felt it clench, then bubble. Was acutely aware of its contents rising. He ran from the foyer to the bathroom.

Once again, he bent over the toilet. And again, he barely raised the lid in time before the mostly liquid gorge sprayed from his mouth. The majority of the vomit made its way into the bowl, but some of it found the floor beside it, some of it landed on the seat. And he could see there was dried puke already collecting where this new watery spew had hit.

Had he been throwing up all night? He didn't recall. Just as he didn't recall putting on the robe and slippers he was wearing. Or placing a blade against his legs and shaving them.

Rising, turning, wiping water from his eyes, wiping saliva and vomit from his chin, Melvin stared into the mirror. Mrs. Thames was right, he didn't look so good.

His eyes were hollowed pits in his face, the left one still mostly red; there was grey around them, bags beneath them. His skin was pale; the hair surrounding his bald spot was disheveled, standing up in all directions as though it were attempting to fly free from his head despite being rooted there. He thought he saw the beginnings of a cold sore opening on his upper lip, something that only happened when he became severely stressed.

At that moment, Lucy entered the bathroom, hopped up on the vanity, and looked in the mirror alongside Melvin. She stared at herself, at him as well, doing so as though understanding she was looking at a pair of reflections. It was something he had never seen her do.

She looked better than she had in months. She had regained nearly all the weight she had lost, her fur was fuller, her eyes more alert than they had ever been. More aware as well. He took solace in her improvement as he observed her in the mirror. Until he had a ghastly thought:

Does Lucy getting better mean I have to get worse?

It was an illogical concern, he told himself. Their lives, their health, were not interconnected in such a way. There was no teetertotter of illness that he shared with his feline family. No, he just hadn't been taking care of himself, hadn't been eating well... or eating at all. He couldn't remember the last time he'd had a meal that wasn't broth and toast.

But he had no appetite for food at the moment. He was too worried about what he had seen in the paper. Now that the sensation of illness had momentarily left his stomach it seemed to travel back up to his mind. He could almost feel the worry gnawing at his brain.

He didn't feel so good, and he wasn't hungry, but he thought maybe there was something in the kitchen that could make him feel better. Something that had always worked pretty well for his mother.

Melvin rinsed out his mouth, took another look at Lucy, then at himself – at the diminishing man reflected back at him – and headed for the kitchen.

47

Melvin sat at his mother's table wearing his mother's robe and slippers. He had placed two of her favourite items on the table before sitting there.

He opened one of them, a bottle of Maria Cristina, the only wine Moira kept in her cabinet. He poured the reddish-purple liquid into the glass she had been drinking from since he had been a child.

Melvin wasn't a drinker. All the times he had walked into this kitchen as a little boy, an adolescent, an adult, and seen his mother sitting at this table, in this seat, reading her trashy books or staring into space, never allowing her glass to remain empty for much longer than it took to fill it, had put him off the idea of drinking.

He had never felt more miserable than on the occasions when she would call him to the kitchen to speak at him, to insult him. To remind him that he had ruined her. He loathed seeing the big purple bottle that stained her tongue and teeth its same colour. A purple tongue wagging between purple teeth, reaching out and lashing him. But she had always seemed like she was enjoying herself.

"But I won't be mean to you, little Lucy. We're gonna have a fun day," he said to himself as well as his cat who was laying on the table in front of him. She looked up briefly at the sound of her name before going back to napping.

"We're gonna have a fun day," he said again, this time in a whisper, before bringing the glass to his lips. He drank, enjoying the sweetness, almost immediately feeling a bit of a rush to his head, and a buzz building in his body as he imbibed on an entirely empty stomach.

He remembered then that it was because of this wine, this glass, and the monster his mother turned into when she drank the former from the latter, that he had Lucy at all.

It had happened on one of those many days that she had called him to the kitchen for no reason other than to insult him. She had been as drunk as he had ever seen her on that particular afternoon. Her eyes watery, her face red, her shoulders swaying, the table and her robe stained with spots and splashes of wine that either hadn't made it into her glass or into her mouth.

Perhaps she had been set off by something in one of her romance novels – maybe a successful young protagonist had reminded her that her son was unsuccessful and growing old in the basement beneath her. More likely, it had been some racy plotline that caused her to begrudge the chance for true romance she felt she had been robbed of since Melvin had been born.

Whatever it was that had set her off had caused her to, out of the blue, tell him to stand in front of her at the table while she recounted the ways he had ruined both her life and his. Slurring as she reiterated, yet again, that he was retarded, that he should have been aborted. That he was the result of a series of ill-omened events, and therefore he must have been cursed. Or he must have been *her* curse. She had told him that she didn't know what she had done to be so unlucky in life, or who she had wronged in a previous life to wind up with a son like him in this one.

He had stood there, taking it, as he always did. Listened without retorting or defending himself, as he always did. He had cried, as he always did, despite trying his hardest not to. Because the sight of his tears always made her smile. And hers was a smile he never enjoyed seeing. But he saw it that day, when she said the things she always said, and he responded the way he always had.

He left the kitchen and the house not long after seeing that sadistic smile, and did something he had never done before. On that afternoon roughly twelve years ago, he had decided to end it all.

Alone, tired of everything, a thirty-year-old Melvin Cockburn had wound up wandering through his neighbourhood until he had reached a wooded trail behind a row of houses. A trail cutting into a few square kilometres of grass and trees. It ran across that grass and through those trees to a river, bringing him to a place called Two Birds Bridge.

He had planned to jump. Had stood at the highest point of the bridge. With his hands on the railing, Melvin had looked over the side at the deepest part of the river. From that height, he likely would have crashed against the rocks beneath the water and been swept away.

He had clearly pictured his body washed up on the rocky sand of the riverbank, feasted on by all the creatures of the woods before being found. His was a body that no one would be in a rush to locate, because he was a person that no one would miss; his mother had made that clear to him.

Melvin had begun to hoist himself up onto the railing when he heard an animal in distress. The sound was coming from the trees near the bridge, not far from the water underneath it. It had been a little cat, meowing mournfully.

Following the sound, he had found Lucy where the trees met the riverbank. She had been injured, cuts and scratches all over her body, her left front paw badly bloodied, looking as if it had been chewed upon by an animal larger than her.

He didn't think about it at all before he scooped her up. He took her home before eventually taking her to South Saturn Animal Hospital that afternoon.

It hadn't been cheap to save her then, but he had been able to afford it with the savings from his piggy bank. He had been adding to it – a quarter, a loony, a five at a time – for the previous twenty-five years. When he had officially adopted the recuperating cat, he had named her Lucy after Lucille Ball, the star of the show *I Love Lucy,* on account of the cat's orange coat. It had been one of his favourite programs as a kid. Melvin had spent many hours entertained by reruns of the popular '50s show, distracted by the misadventures of the ginger-haired Lucy, her husband Ricardo, and their neighbours Ethel and Fred. He had wished even then that he could drift into their world and live there instead of in his.

For the next dozen years after Lucy had made a full recovery, she had been his best friend. She had been the only reason he hadn't jumped off Two Birds Bridge, as many had before him. She was the reason he was still alive. The memory was bittersweet. It would have been entirely bitter if Lucy was still dying.

But she isn't, he reminded himself, allowing himself to relax. Looking at her fondly (without that stupid onesie covering her!), smiling at her, he knew she now had hope. She had a chance, no matter how unusual her circumstances were.

That was worth drinking to.

Before long, the first glass was gone, then a second, a third. The entire while, Melvin grinned while staring at the blinds covering the window of the back door. He stared through them, into the yard. He looked through the recently dug ground, into the dual grave he had made for his mother and her helper boy. The grave he had covered with her precious petunias. He pictured the two of them in there.

He chuckled at the memory of burying Moira and Brian. He laughed as he recalled how he had positioned them, face to face, crotch to crotch, like lovers.

They deserve each other, he thought. *They deserve what they got.*

"Who's laughing now, cunt?" he said, then stuck out his tongue in their direction, making a razzing sound a toddler might have giggled at and tried to emulate.

He looked down at his tongue, stuck it to the side so his nose wasn't obstructing his view, and saw that it was purple. He pictured his teeth being coloured much the same. Looking down at his purple tongue while wearing his mother's pale peach robe, sitting at her table, in her seat, he suddenly found the situation not only funny but hilarious.

Melvin could barely maintain his composure as he spoke past the door and all the way into the shallow grave he had dug. He spoke at his dead mother as she had always done to him. In his best impression of his favourite comedian, Jerry Seinfeld, he said,

"Looks like *I* aborted *you!*"

Melvin cackled then. Let loose bursts of laughter equating to a fit. He guffawed until he worried he might not be able to stop. Continuing to stare through the door, he laughed until his sides hurt.

But he did indeed feel better.

48

Upon waking the next morning, Melvin felt just about as sick as he could ever recall feeling. On top of the nausea that had been plaguing him over the last week or so, his tongue was Sahara dry, his stomach pained him, and he had a splitting headache.

The headache was only made worse by the ringing of the doorbell that had woken him up.

He briefly had the thought that it might be some solicitor, a door-to-door salesman. And the idea of that made him feel uneasy for reasons he couldn't quite understand. He tried to ignore the bell, but the person at the door didn't seem to want to go away.

Eventually, after lifting a head that suddenly seemed heavier than it had been his entire adult life, he dragged his weary body from the living room, where he had fallen asleep, to the front door. But before opening it, he remembered the mistake he had made the last time.

Melvin looked down at himself, and was once again stunned to see that he had changed his clothes at some point during the night. He was now wearing the outfit he had taken from Mr. Gorman's closet after murdering the man and his wife. He had no memory of switching from his mom's robe and slippers to Mr. Gorman's collared shirt and jeans. And, as he strained to think back to the day before, he realized that he didn't remember anything after sitting at the table and drinking his mother's wine. He was confused, worried for himself.

The person at the door rang again. More than anything, Melvin and his pounding headache wanted them to stop.

"Better than a girly robe," he reasoned, coming to terms with his change of clothing before opening the front door. And finding himself face to face with two uniformed police officers.

"Melvin Cockburn?" one officer – a tall white male with a buzzcut and a barrel for a chest – said, mispronouncing Melvin's name while looking at a small pad of paper. Melvin's unending rage at the common mispronunciation helped to steady his nerves, but only slightly. He was doing his best not to shake while willing the sweat to push itself back into his pores, thankful for the cool breeze that greeted him along with these members of law enforcement.

Melvin nodded in response to the question, indicating he was the person they were looking for. He crossed his arms tightly over his chest, as if somehow that would hide the fact that he was wearing a dead man's clothes.

"I'm officer Dobbins, this is officer Kent. Is Moira Cockburn home?" the other officer said, a woman with a dirty blonde ponytail and a body made of wiry muscle. She also mispronounced his surname. Melvin had to fight the urge to correct them.

"My mom? No, she's not here," he said, remembering the lie he'd told the detective who had called him the other morning. "She took a trip to see a sick friend. Did she break the law?" Melvin said, asking the question as a joke, attempting to add some humour to the conversation in hopes that he would appear more innocent than he felt.

Neither of the officers laughed nor offered a hint of a smile.

"We wanted to talk to you about what happened across the street. At the Gorman house," Barrel Chest said.

Melvin felt his sphincter tighten, the buttocks around it clench. He had already been leaning against the doorframe, but was now consciously appreciative of the support it gave him, because his knees had weakened all at once.

"The Gormans, yes. Such a terrible thing to hear about," Melvin said, hoping he sounded sympathetic, convincing, but already imagining a ride in handcuffs, a life behind bars. A life without Lucy.

"We're canvassing the area just to see if anyone noticed anything of note. In the last week, have you noticed any peculiar persons lurking around? Any cars parked where they shouldn't have been? Or anything you found strange in the neighbourhood leading up to the murders? Have you or your mother ever known the Gormans to have any enemies or recent altercations?" the female officer, Dobbins, asked in a flurry.

The questions made Melvin feel a measure of relief that bordered on euphoria. They weren't here for him or looking for his mother, they were just canvassing. The police were desperate for answers because they didn't have any.

"The Gormans? Enemies? Gosh, no. They are..." he quickly scanned his brain to recall the words Mrs. Thames had said on the news, "...They *were* the life of the street. Always having a good time. So many laughs with those two," he said, doing his best impression of a sad neighbour by imitating what he had seen of his sincerely sad neighbour on TV. When the two officers only stood there, as though they expected him to say more, Melvin added, "And no, I didn't notice anything out of the ordinary. Just... it's so scary that this sort of thing could have happened in our neighbourhood."

The male officer jotted a few notes in his pad, the female officer didn't take her eyes off Melvin, obviously scrutinizing him – how ill he looked, how his clothes didn't quite fit him. He did his best not to shake as he worried if this might end up being more than just a routine canvassing of the Gormans' neighbours, after all.

"Thank you for your time, sir. Try to get some rest. You don't look so well," said the male officer. Melvin's buttocks unclenched in his relief.

"Y-you're welcome," he replied, damning the little stutter in his voice. "Have a good day," he added more steadily. "And good luck!"

Dobbins turned to look at him again, even as they walked away. Her stare was that of a jury foreman about to read a guilty verdict. Suddenly, the breeze he felt wasn't cool, it was icy.

Waving at her timidly, Melvin ducked back into his house, closing the door behind him. He leaned against the closed door, allowed his weak knees to give, and he slid down until he was sitting on the ground, his head in his hands, his body shaking violently as he fought against tears and another bout of sickness.

From the kitchen, Lucy meowed, announcing to Melvin that it was time for her to eat again.

49

Melvin sat there with his back against the door for a time that felt immeasurable. It passed slowly and heavily, each tick of the clock adding to the gravity in the room, making the air itself feel heavier, making his mind feel weighted.

Adding to that burden was the sound of his cat's voice, crying that she was hungry, insisting on being fed, demanding that Melvin be the one to provide her what she needed.

"*How*, Lucy? I... *I can't!* Didn't you see how crazy it was out there the other night? Didn't you see how many people are already suspicious? I just... *How?*"

He banged the back of his head against the door in anger. And nearly leapt to his feet when he heard the door respond.

It was someone knocking.

No, not again! Melvin thought. He wanted to ignore it, but he feared he had already been heard.

"Mr. Cockburn?" said a gravelly male voice from outside. "Is everything okay?"

And there was the confirmation that Melvin had indeed been heard. He could no longer simply sit there and ignore this unwelcome visitor.

At least he pronounced my name right, Melvin thought warily. Feeling defeated, he rose to his feet and opened the door.

And found himself looking at another police officer.

Even though the man was not wearing a uniform, it was obvious to Melvin that he was law enforcement. He stood with the air of someone visiting in an official capacity. He had short, slicked back, mostly grey hair that had once been brown. Below that hair was a clean-shaven face which was wrinkled with ruddy skin. In the middle of that wrinkled and ruddy face was a nose that betrayed his bad habit. It was a drunkard's nose, swollen, misshapen, and full of broken capillaries.

Melvin's visitor was dressed in an outfit which included grey slacks, a white shirt, and a loosened navy-blue necktie. He reeked of authority. He reeked of cigarette smoke as well.

Melvin wasn't surprised when he saw this man reach into the inside of his brown tweed coat to remove a badge from his breast pocket, exposing the firearm on his right hip as he did so. Purposely, Melvin believed.

"I'm Detective William Kelly," the large, square jawed, slightly overweight man said. He reminded Melvin of an old bear, a grizzled grizzly, a creature that had once been grand and majestic, but was now diminished as all things are when touched long enough by the hands of time. And, like an old bear, the man may not have been what he once was, but he looked like he still had the potential of being dangerous, deadly, if provoked.

"Oh," Melvin replied, the name not registering immediately although the voice sounded familiar. It was like stone rubbing against stone. "I just spoke to two officers about what happened across the street. I didn't see anything out of the norm."

The man looked over his shoulder at the house decorated in yellow tape as though he hadn't been aware of the double homicide committed there.

"Sad what people are capable of," Detective Kelly said, almost to himself. "But I'm not here because of your neighbours. Not *those* neighbours, anyhow. We spoke over the phone about your former neighbour, Brian Norton. The young man who went missing several days ago. Remember? You said your mom was in Montreal, but you would reach out to her to see if she knew anything. I'm hoping she might be back, or you might give me her contact number. As it stands, she may have been the last person who saw Mr. Norton. His family would truly appreciate it if I could speak with her."

"She's not... Hey! I didn't say you could come in!"

But the brazen cop had already shouldered his way past Melvin, who, experiencing a sense of déjà vu, scrambled to get back in front of him before he could walk further into the house. He found himself standing face to face (specifically, forehead to chin) with the gruff, burly lawman in the foyer. From this distance, without the breeze of the outdoors between them, Melvin could smell the faint aroma of whiskey on his breath.

Great. Not just a cop, but a liquored-up cop.

"I told you, officer," Melvin said, patiently, fearfully, "I don't know anything about where Brian went. And my mom and I aren't exactly close, so she doesn't really call to check in. When she comes back, I'll get her to call you."

Detective Kelly only stood there, swaying slightly as he looked Melvin up and down.

"Something stinks," he said. Initially, Melvin believed he was referring to what Melvin had said; he thought the detective didn't believe his story. But he saw, as the detective waved a hand in front of his nose in disgust, that he meant there was an actual foul odour in the house. Something Melvin couldn't smell at all.

"Well, I'm sure it's not a crime for you to not like the way my house smells. I really can't help you, sir."

"You see, I'm not sure if that's true. I'm not sure if anything you've told me so far is true," the greying detective said, looking around the house as if he might find some evidence to confirm his suspicions at a glance.

He doesn't know anything, Melvin realized, feeling a minor measure of relief. He believed this detective to be some rogue cop at the end of his rope, grasping at straws, hoping for a clue he could report to his superiors to convince them that he shouldn't be forced into retirement. Did those superiors even know he was here, harassing a private citizen and barging into a home without welcome or warrant?

But he knows enough... Or suspects enough to be here. It's only a matter of time before he figures out that he'll never hear from my mom. Then he'll get his warrant, and it won't matter if I welcome him in here or not, he and a bunch of cops will be all over this place. How long before they see that the flowers are all dug up? How long before they're out there digging up mom and Brian?

"Really, what *is* that smell?" the detective inquired, irritation apparent in his voice, as though offended that the smell was accosting him. Again, he pushed past Melvin, taking several steps into the hall, toward the kitchen and living area where he thought whatever he smelled must be coming from.

Melvin followed frantically, taking short, rapid steps in comparison to the detective's long casual strides. Melvin was wondering how to stop him when Detective Kelly stopped on his own.

His attention had been snared by one of the framed images on the hallway wall. It was an enlarged black and white photo of Melvin's mother back in her heyday. This was the image she had always referred to while telling Melvin that his birth had ruined a nearly perfect body. In it, Moira Cockburn was jean clad from neck to ankle, wearing a sleeveless jean jacket, and skin-tight dark denim pants. She was straddling a motorcycle with a cigarette in her mouth.

The right side of Detective Kelly's body was angled toward Melvin as he inspected the photo. Melvin was staring at the officer's coat-covered right hip, upon which was his pistol.

Detective Kelly whistled at the picture.

"This your mom?" he asked, a lascivious smile on his face, further wrinkling it, making it appear ruddier. The smile was in his voice as well, causing the old man to sound younger, like he might have sounded two hundred thousand cigarettes ago. He continued to gawk at the young version of Moira Cockburn.

"She was one *fine* piece... Reminds me of a girl I pulled over for speeding when I was just a kid in uniform. No, that ain't right. She wuddn't a girl, she was a *woman*. She had at least fifteen years on me. That must have been... oh, maybe forty years ago now? Fuck, how time flies... I was set to give her a ticket 'til she promised to show me a good time instead." He chuckled at the fond memory. "Mouth like one of them Dyson vacuums, that one. Pussy like wet velvet. That was one of the best nights of my life," he added wistfully before ripping his eyes from the photo and turning back to the kitchen.

Melvin might have recognized this rendition of a familiar story had he been paying attention, but he hadn't been. He wasn't. His focus was on one thing: closing the gap between him and Detective Kelly as the lawman continued to saunter, uninvited, into Melvin's house.

Now he was at the entrance of the kitchen. Was looking into it. And that was when Detective Kelly stopped again.

Melvin continued walking up to him, knowing that the cop was looking at the table. Looking at Lucy laying upon it.

"Sweet Mary, Mother of God!" Detective Kelly rumbled, though his words were muffled by his right hand, which was covering his mouth, leaving his right hip exposed. "What the fuck is wrong wi–

Melvin lunged for the cop's hip. For his sidearm. He didn't think about what he was doing, or what the potential consequences of his actions might be if they proved unsuccessful. All he could think about was that this man had to be eliminated. He couldn't have him snooping around, making Melvin's life miserable until he finally figured out enough of what was going on to arrest him. To take him away from Lucy.

"Hey!" the detective roared, reaching both for Melvin's hands and his pistol at once. Detective Kelly was larger and stronger, but Melvin was faster, younger, more desperate. Sober. And after a panicked second, during which his hands were tangled in the cop's jacket, he managed to yank the gun free of the holster and the jacket just before Detective Kelly's large, slow, drunken hands got to where they needed to be. By the time those meaty paws slapped down on his hip, Melvin already had the gun pointed at the detective. He began taking several steps backward, toward the front door.

He didn't stop until he was near the entrance, feeling a slight breeze coming through the ajar door at his back. He had put the entire hallway between him and the overbearing lawman, giving himself plenty of space to aim and shoot. Most importantly, the distance between them made it impossible for Detective Kelly to grab and disarm him like cops always seemed able to do on TV.

"Are you fucking crazy?" the detective huffed, though he did not look scared. He straightened his jacket, took a step forward, extended his hand as if expecting the pistol to be gently placed in it. Detective Kelly, like most people Melvin had encountered throughout his life, wasn't taking him seriously at all. "There are police officers canvasing the neighbourhood right now. There's law enforcement right across the street. What do you really think you're gonna do with that thing?"

Melvin answered by pulling the trigger.

50

Life, for a moment, paused as Melvin squeezed the death device. He waited for an explosion, a blast.

All he heard was a click.

Both men realized at the same time that the safety mechanism of the pistol was still engaged. With that realization, life unpaused. Began to play at hyperspeed.

Melvin had no idea where the safety mechanism was and how to turn it off. And he knew he wasn't going to get much of a chance to figure it out.

Detective Kelly, sensing the opportunity, charged at Melvin. Fists pumping, head low and jutted forward, he was a raging bull to a matador's cape.

Melvin fumbled with the gun; he wanted to look at it and find the safety but didn't want to take his eyes off the approaching officer of the law, the detective who was twenty steps away.

Fifteen steps.

The gap was nearly closed.

Melvin, abandoning the idea of shooting this man with his own gun, instead reared his arm back. He did his best impression of Roger Clements, Pedro Martinez, Nolan Ryan, the way he sometimes did when watching a particularly exciting game and fantasizing about playing a sport his mother had never allowed him to as a child; pretending, in those lonely moments, that he was anyone but himself. Channelling those pitchers, Melvin hurled the gun like a baseball as hard as he was able.

The weapon hit Detective Kelly squarely between the eyes.

It bounced off his face and ricocheted to the ground. Melvin flinched and shielded his head when the gun clattered, fearing it would accidentally discharge and shoot him. That's the way it always went in the movies and television shows. But life did not imitate art on this occasion, much to Melvin's relief.

He turned his attention back to the intruder in his house. To his chagrin, he saw that Detective Kelly wasn't unconscious. The man was still on his feet but was visibly stunned. Stumbling backward, he held one hand pressed against his forehead where the gun had hit him. His other hand was extended toward the wall, groping for it in an effort to maintain his balance.

This time, it was Maple Leafs enforcer Tie Domi that Melvin channelled as he launched himself at the off-balance officer. He hit him shoulder first, right in the middle of his body, sending him flying into the wall near the entrance to the kitchen like Domi might send an opponent flying into the boards while patrolling the ice.

The detective nearly went through the wall, creating a man-shaped dent in it, sending drywall crashing down in dusty pieces. He then fell to the floor, dust flying up above him, gypsum falling on his head.

But he remained conscious. The hand that had been reaching for the wall earlier was now pressed against the ground, attempting to raise him to his feet. Melvin couldn't have that.

He grabbed the gun from the floor.

Strode swiftly to the fallen cop.

In his hand, the gun became a hammer. And this man's head became a nail.

Melvin brought the gun down several times. Raised it and lowered it repeatedly until he heard a crunch, saw parted skin. He continued connecting the butt of the gun with the top of Detective Kelly's head until that parted skin released blood. In spurts, in bursts, in geysers. The entire while, Lucy was meowing of her hunger from the kitchen.

When Melvin was done his bludgeoning, after taking a moment to steady his breathing, to calm his heart, he dragged the unconscious detective into the kitchen, toward the sound of his cat's voice.

To an area in which he would have more space to prepare Lucy's next meal.

51

Melvin had two major issues on his hands. The first was that he had a naked and unconscious police detective on his kitchen floor while other police officers milled around the house across the street from his. The second issue was that he had run out of the duct tape necessary to ensure the detective remained immobile.

Melvin needed a way to keep Detective Kelly on the floor, unmoving. But he had no tape nor rope, nothing with which to bind a person's limbs. He had used most of his tape on his mother and Brian. The last couple of strips had gone toward taping over Detective Kelly's mouth after having shoved a sock inside it.

Melvin had stripped the detective of his clothes after bludgeoning him and dragging him into the kitchen. He had done his best to avoid getting blood on the garments; a task which proved to be futile given how much had gushed from the man's skull as Melvin had battered him. But the clothes hadn't been completely ruined, which was a blessing to Melvin. He would need them for later. For his escape.

As he paced around the prone detective and thought about his clothes and what to do with his naked body, Melvin realized he had overlooked something that might help him. He had forgotten to check Detective Kelly's pockets. There, he hoped he would find half of the solution to his problems.

He turned toward the kitchen table, upon which Lucy sat watching the events unravel, yowling her encouragement, reminding him of her appetite, of her need to heal. On one of the chairs were the detective's pants, shirt, undergarments, jacket.

Melvin checked the jacket first and found he had chosen wisely. After discovering a flask and the officer's badge in one of the interior breast pockets, he found what he was looking for in the other: a pair of handcuffs and a key.

He wasted no time running back to Detective Kelly, rolling him onto his stomach, wrenching his large, limp arms behind his back, and fumbling with the cuffs and the officer's wrists before managing to wrap the metal bracelets around them. He cinched the cuffs tight enough for the surrounding skin to swell and redden, then he rolled the lawman onto his back, pinning his arms beneath him. It was a good way to subdue a person, Melvin thought as he evaluated his work.

But it wasn't enough.

He looked lower on the body – past a short, thick penis poking out of an enormous bush of salt and pepper pubic hair – at Detective Kelly's legs. How would he restrain those? If he got to his feet, this cop could likely take Melvin on even with his hands bound. Melvin was ill, weakened, and worn down.

Thinking, stressing, pacing, with his cat practically screaming at him from the table, Melvin became aware that he had run out of time. That the time for thinking was over, the time for acting was now. Because, from the floor, out of the bloody head of Detective Kelly, came a long, mournful, painfilled groan.

There was a movement of the legs, a wriggling of the shoulders, a shifting of the body. He was barely conscious, yet he was already trying to get to his feet.

Melvin acted quickly, not thinking. Or perhaps, in the back of his mind, he had known that what he was about to do had been the answer all along. And was only now, when things were desperate, acknowledging that it couldn't be avoided.

He took two steps, one of them a lunge, before he leapt.

In his mind, while in the air, he was a basketballer flying to the rim. He was Dominique Wilkins, Spud Webb, Michael Jordan. He was 'Chocolate Thunder' Darryl Dawkins. But when he came down, he was nothing so graceful. He was no longer a man but a two-footed wrecking ball.

He had aimed both of those feet at the knees of Detective Kelly, and came crashing down on the middle of the lawman's legs. He was nearly made sick by the cracking sounds he heard despite hoping he would hear them.

He fell awkwardly to the floor, right beside the writhing, groaning man whose screams were trapped in his mouth by the sock stuffed in it. Melvin, nearly spent, rolled over and away from Detective Kelly, worried he might squirm his way over and butt Melvin with his head. Or pin him down, holding Melvin still with nothing but the weight of his body. But Melvin's movement was unnecessary. Detective Kelly was in too much pain to pay attention to him. The cop was dealing with two badly broken legs.

Melvin scrambled to his feet, and, despite not wanting to, in spite of knowing better, he looked down at the mess he had made of this man's legs. He immediately looked away, bent over and retched, though nothing escaped from his stomach.

With his eyes closed, Melvin tried to recover his breath. He saw the detective's legs clearly in his mind, as though he had never turned away from them. The horror of those shattered limbs would forever be seared into his brain. There would be no avoiding them, even if he never saw them again. With that in mind, Melvin opened his eyes and slowly turned back to the naked detective thrashing in pain on the floor. Forced himself to gaze again upon those decimated lower limbs.

The injury might not have been as bad had the backs of Detective Kelly's legs been flat against the floor when

Melvin had leapt on them. But, because he had been partially propped up by the cuffed hands behind his back, his knees had been given just enough space to be stomped in the wrong direction. The damage was catastrophic.

The backs of his knees touched the floor while his shins were kicking up, aimed in the opposite direction, resting at awkward angles. It was a position that should have been impossible for the human body. The kneecap of the right leg, the one closest to Melvin, was visible from the side of the leg where it had shifted.

But that wasn't the worst of it.

What he was most concerned about was the blood that was beginning to pool under Detective Kelly. From the backs of his knees, where broken bones had burst through the skin and had cut some sort of vein or artery in the process based on the amount of blood he was losing.

"Fuuuuuck," Melvin whispered, angry with himself, understanding what losing that much blood meant. And if he hadn't understood it on his own, Lucy was on the table at his back, howling the meaning at him. Telling him to hurry up before there was no blood left. Before the heart pumping that blood would stop beating.

"Okay, Lucy! God, I get it! Stop yelling at me!"

Detective Kelly was a writhing mess on the floor, blood beneath his head and legs, his hands bound behind him, he moaned into his gag as he stared up at Melvin with pain-fevered eyes. He squirmed on the ground like an earthworm in the mud, well aware of birds descending. There was nothing he could do to get away.

With one of his issues resolved, Melvin retrieved his mother's knife from its block on the counter. Satisfied with how sharp it was, he marched toward the cuffed and gagged and writhing cop.

52

Melvin put the knife into Detective Kelly's skin. The bound and broken man screamed into his gag and did his best to shift his body, but Melvin knelt on the detective's lower belly and across his hips in order to keep him as still as possible. To keep safe the heart Lucy so sorely needed. Wanting to drown out the muffled sound of Detective Kelly's sock and duct tape filtered wails, Melvin spoke nervously as he cut.

"I know what you're thinking. It's just like you said before, there are a million officers out there looking for me. But they don't know it's me they're looking for. And they won't find me. Because first, I'll be you..."

Melvin sliced into his midsection, parted the flesh of the torso down the center, from breast to belly button, and was now spreading the wound wider, cutting through the viscera and diaphragm, creating the pathway he needed.

He looked at Detective Kelly's face, hoping the man would be unconscious. Unfortunately, he wasn't. His screams were now soft moans, his eyes had begun to glaze over. But they were still alert enough for Melvin to be certain the detective understood him.

"I'll wear your clothes and take your car and be out of here before anyone knows what's going on. *Then* I'll be my mom. Understand? I have her hats and her clothes... You should have seen me in her robe; my neighbour actually thought I *was* her." He laughed nervously as he put the knife down before reaching into the dying man's body. A body which was no longer fighting or shifting but was still and accepting as Melvin pushed his hand into the messy, wet warmth of Detective Kelly's chest.

"I have her credit cards, her bank card, her cash. I'll get a ticket to somewhere far where no one will catch me. Lucy and I will go on doing what we have to do to survive."

He was inside the man up to his forearm, reaching for his heart, when he thought he heard Detective Kelly attempting to speak.

Melvin stopped his work, looked at the butchered man, and found that he was not looking back at Melvin but over his shoulder, at Lucy on the table. And, indeed, he was trying to speak, making a series of noises that sounded like they might have been words had he not been gagged. Melvin considered removing the tape and sock as he had with his mother, but it was then that Detective Kelly lost consciousness. And whatever he had been trying to say was taken into the darkness with him.

Worried the man might be dead, Melvin reached further into the torso, and was relieved to feel the heart beating. He wrapped his hand around it and began to pull and twist, pinching off connecting pieces, wrenching on the organ until it was free.

Just as he had with his mother's heart, he approached Lucy at the table with care, expediency, fear, like a servant bringing food to a finicky master, unsure of what their reaction might be. Unsure if the food would be accepted once it reached the one waiting to be served.

Melvin was worried that the heart might stop before it got to Lucy. He was concerned that she might reject a dead heart and be made worse for it. But when he sat down on one of the chairs, and presented the bloody muscle to his best friend, it was still faintly pulsating in his palms. And Lucy was eager to receive it.

More life, Melvin thought as Lucy pounced on the heart in his hands. He felt it gradually slow, then stop beating, as she bit and ripped and chewed. He closed his eyes. Too tired to move from the chair, not wanting to disrupt his cat's feeding, he sat there with a diminishing heart in his hands, attempting to block out the growling guttural noises coming from his cat, hoping it would soon be over. Not only this particular meal, but the entire ordeal; the attacking of people, the cutting of them, the killing of them. This was not what he wanted for his future.

A future as a fugitive. The thought was a cold current in his consciousness, causing him a chill.

Melvin went over his plan several times as he fed his cat, recounting in his mind the details he had described to the now dead detective on his floor. He convinced himself it would all work without a hitch. But for that to be true, he urged himself, he would have to get going as soon as he cleaned himself up.

Lucy had eaten nearly the entire heart. Melvin felt her tongue licking at his palms, was tickled by her teeth as she tried to salvage every portion.

"This has to be the last one," he whispered to Lucy, wanting desperately for this to be true, hoping that once she finished this heart, her tumour would be completely and permanently healed, and she would be back to normal. Back to not needing life to live. Melvin couldn't imagine where he would find another victim. The idea of going out and killing a stranger again sickened him, and he didn't expect candidates for Lucy's meals to continue falling into his lap the way they had so far.

When Lucy was done eating, she backed away from his bloody hands, walked a circle on the table, and lay down satisfied.

Melvin couldn't help but smile as he watched her, knowing she was getting better even as she lay there. He stood, intending to go to the sink and wash the remnants of the detective's heart and insides from his hands and arms. After that, he planned to change into

Detective Kelly's clothes, pack some bags, collect his cat, and leave shortly thereafter. But he never made it to the sink.

He had barely moved in his seat when he realized that clean hands were the last thing he needed to worry about. Because, as he turned from the table, he saw that he was not alone.

Standing there, in the entranceway between the kitchen and the hall, looking stricken, ashen, shocked, and, worst of all, looking like she might attempt to run away, was Melvin's favourite neighbour, Mrs. Chloe Thames.

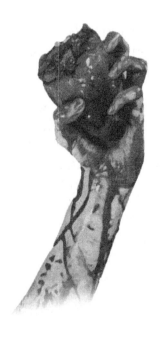

53

"I was just... I was just... I couldn't find Obi... I thought he might be in your yard again, and I heard strange noises, and the front door wasn't closed... and, and, and... Please, Melvin, I... I just want to find my dog. I didn't see anything."

It was the most out of sorts Melvin could remember Mrs. Thames ever being. Even after the tragic disappearances of her son and husband, she had always seemed composed. Now she was rambling, stumbling through her sentences. Her hands were up, palms open, to indicate surrender. As though she expected him to pounce on her at any moment.

And she was right to expect that, Melvin thought, feeling ill again. He would have to pounce on her. He couldn't let her leave. He couldn't let her put an end to Lucy's successful recovery. Because, despite her saying she hadn't seen anything, she had seen too much.

The kitchen was a pool. And it seemed as though Detective Kelly was afloat in it. From the edge of the table where Melvin sat, to the entranceway where Mrs. Thames stood, a body between them, the entire floor was red. Yes, she had seen far too much.

"Mrs. Thames, I..." How could he explain this? How could he calm her down so she wouldn't flee?

He looked around the room, attempted to see things as she might be seeing them now. A naked corpse on the ground, its legs broken so badly the bones poked out from the backs of them, its midsection opened up nearly from chest to waist, many of its insides currently out of it.

Including the remnants of heart in Melvin's hands.

"I'm just..." Melvin tried again, still not knowing what to say before deciding on the truth, as crazy as he knew it sounded. "I'm just feeding my cat... I know it seems strange, but I can explain. You see, my cat is sick..."

"Oh my God! It was *you!* It was *you* who killed the Gormans!" Mrs. Thames screamed.

So much for keeping her calm, Melvin thought as his neighbour alternated her panicked stare from Melvin's face to the mostly eaten heart in his hands. She took a slow step away from him, then another step, even slower, in the direction of the hall. In the direction of the front door. It was as though she had stumbled upon a wild animal, some apex predator, and believed that if she moved too quickly, too suddenly, it might spring up, biting and clawing. Turning her into something resembling the body on the floor.

"Poor Jill and Dan, you..." Melvin watched Mrs. Thames's face contort, amalgamating revulsion and revelation. "You... Jesus Christ, *you ate their hearts...*" she finally said. It was a whisper from a woman struck nearly dumb by awe and terror.

"No! Of course not! That was Lucy. She needs... Listen, I know it's going to sound crazy, but she needs the hearts to survive. I had to feed them to her to save her. You can understand that, can't you? Wouldn't you do the same for Obi?" Melvin reasoned. Though he knew he sounded unreasonable, beyond reason. Which was exactly how Mrs. Thames regarded him, like a man who had long since parted ways with rationality.

"But your cat..." She looked from him to the kitchen table behind him, her face displaying dismay, disbelief, disgust. Dread. "Melvin... Your cat is dead."

"Dead? What?" He looked back at Lucy on the table.

This time it was his face that contorted with all the emotions he had read on the countenance of Mrs. Thames.

Something had gone wrong. Maybe the detective's old booze and cigarette infested heart had been bad. That had to be it. He couldn't imagine anything else being the cause of what he was seeing.

Because, while only moments ago, Lucy had been sleeping on the table looking as content and healthy as she had ever looked, now she was sick again. The worst she had ever been.

She was laying there motionless. From his vantage he could see her chest, and the gaping tumour which took up far too much of that area. The tumour that was now overwhelmed by flies, gnats, and crawling things he couldn't identify, all eating at the puss and blood that filled it. He saw those same insects crawling over her stiff and shrunken body from her tail to the tip of her nose. Still, Melvin wouldn't believe it.

"No... She's just tired, and sick, bu–"

The sound of Mrs. Thames turning and running snatched his attention from the confusing condition of his cat. He would have to help Lucy later.

Letting out an aggravated groan, Melvin threw down the remnants of heart he held. He stood, wiping his red hands on his pants while he waded through the blood on the floor until he got to Detective Kelly's body.

He picked up the knife he had left beside it and proceeded to run his favourite neighbour down.

54

"Wait! Mrs. Thames! Mrs. Thames! Wait!"

She wouldn't wait. It was a wonder she had stuck around as long as she had. But she was fleeing now and had a significant head start.

At first, Melvin thought he could catch her despite the lead she had gotten on him. But his stomach was roiling, and he felt as tired as he could ever remember feeling. He was drained from his efforts with Detective Kelly. Sapped by everything he had been going through over these last several days.

She's going to get away, he thought, dismayed, as he watched his neighbour run slowly down the hallway. *She's going to get away and go straight to the police and they'll get me. And no one will be able to save Lucy.*

He let out a growl of rage and exasperation as he attempted to will a sick, unathletic, atrophied body to move faster than it was able.

Mrs. Thames was halfway between Melvin and the door. She would be the entire way there in a matter of seconds. Then she would be out in the world, screaming her head off, letting everyone know that Melvin had done a few bad things to save the life of his best friend. He was in the middle of releasing another frustrated roar when something happened that caused him to quiet.

Mrs. Thames tripped.

Out of nowhere, only feet away from the door, she went from running all out to crumpling to the ground. She crashed knees first, then fell onto her face, barely having the time to throw out her arms to soften her fall.

No, she didn't trip, Melvin thought, remembering their last conversation.

"My doctor says I have to take it easy or else I might reinjure it," Mrs. Thames had said about her recently broken ankle. The ankle she had just reinjured after not following her doctor's orders.

Melvin never imagined he would be gladdened by the sight of Mrs. Thames in pain. But glad was how he felt as he saw her on the floor, now sitting up, clutching an ankle that she was no doubt cursing for betraying her.

Usually, a sight like this would sadden him. Mrs. Thames was the only person Melvin felt sorrier for than himself. A widow, a mourning mother, she was someone who had survived so much mental and physical trauma. But if she got away, she would cause him to lose not only his freedom but his best friend. That was not an option.

"I'm sorry, Mrs. Thames. But I'm doing what I'm doing to save Lucy. I promise I'll make it as quick as I can. And it's not all bad... When it's done, when you're gone, you'll be reunited with your son and your husband, and anyone else you lost."

She let out a moan that was half howl, reminiscent of the wounded animal he had turned her into. It was a sound that indicated the pain she felt at his words rather than the pain emanating from her reinjured ankle.

"Your fucking cat is *DEAD!*" Mrs. Thames shouted. She might have screamed more, but in a matter of seconds Melvin was beside her. Before he thought about it, before he thought at all, he kicked her squarely in the ribs. Harder than he believed he was capable. He hadn't believed he would have been capable of such an act at all. Not to Mrs. Thames. But what she had said had set him off.

"My cat is *NOT* dead!" Melvin raged at her. He looked back in the direction of the kitchen, recalling what he had seen only a minute ago. His cat on the table, her body drawn and desiccated, her coat yellowed, hair hanging limp where it hadn't already fallen off her. Insects crawling all over her...

No, he shook his head, cleared the image. *She's just sick. She just needs the right heart. Yes, that's it! Think about it, Mel. You fed her the heart of your cunt of a mother, then that stupid son of a bitch, Brian. And God knows what that single mother was doing walking the streets at night instead of taking care of her kid. Then it was those two asshole neighbours who spent their time getting drunk and stoned and laughing at nice people who did nothing wrong to them. And then the cop, a drunk pig.* Of course *those hearts couldn't properly heal Lucy. They were bad. But now... now we have a good heart.*

He could almost hear it beating from where he stood above her. The heart of a survivor. Of someone who constantly persevered. It was a heart that had been badly broken but had since healed.

And now it would heal Lucy.

55

Mrs. Thames had made her way onto her hands and knees. Judging by the sounds coming from her, the way her face had reddened, and the bulging veins in her neck and forehead, Melvin had kicked the wind out of her. She gasped, wheezed, cried.

He kicked her again. Not a punt this time but a push with the bottom of his foot. He did this to turn her on her side. Then did it once more to get her onto her back. He proceeded to mount her. With his ass on her abdomen, he used his knees to pin her arms to the floor by her sides. She squirmed, attempted to buck him off her just as Mrs. Gorman had done while she was chained to the bed. But Mrs. Thames had one useless ankle and two deflated lungs. She didn't have the strength to fight even this weakened version of Melvin.

He brought the knife to her chest.

"It'll be quick, I promise," he whispered to her. A lie. With shaky hands attached to an exhausted body, he cut through the thin windbreaker jacket she wore, sliced into her shirt as well. Mrs. Thames gasped as much as her windless lungs would allow as her skin was parted next.

This was the difficult part, keeping them alive while trying to remove from them their hearts. He needed his hands to be steady. He couldn't risk losing this heart – *the* heart – that would finally cure Lucy for good.

But his body shook and lurched, causing his hands, the knife, to do the same. Mrs. Thames squealed, a sad, pathetic noise. Melvin attempted to steady his hands but couldn't. They trembled violently because of what was happening inside of him.

His stomach. It was acting up again.

Before he could think of moving, of attempting to turn his head, Melvin was vomiting. Spraying from his mouth was a mostly liquid spew of reddish discharge.

And this time his mind allowed him to see it for what it was.

Blood mixed with bile, along with chunks of membrane, roughly chewed veins, barely masticated portions of ventricle.

All of it landed directly on Mrs. Thames's face. Into her open mouth. And Melvin wasn't finished.

Surge after surge, the contents of his stomach emptied on his neighbour. A cascade, a crimson waterfall of blood and bile and bits of human heart.

His body hitched, his body heaved. He was no longer in control of it. He found himself falling over, sliding sidelong off Mrs. Thames, his knees no longer on her arms, his ass removed from her abdomen. He teetered until he was no longer atop her but beside her on the floor.

His body wouldn't relent its spasticity. He dry-heaved, twitched. His eyes blurred, wet but burning. Through those eyes, in their contradicting state, he saw Mrs. Thames wiping away the vomit from her face in large, frantic swipes, her mouth spitting out what his had just released. Next, her hands moved down to her chest as they groped for the knife that was stuck inside of her. It protruded from her at an angle, gravity attempting to pull it down by the handle as the tip was wedged firmly in her sternum, perhaps lodged against a bone.

He reached for it as she reached for it.

They both grabbed the handle of the knife at the same time. But he was sick and weak while she had regained her wind and was running on adrenaline and the need to survive. She wrenched the knife from her chest, wrested it away from him.

"M-Mrs. Thames," Melvin wheezed. "Do–"

He meant to say 'don't,' but he didn't. He didn't say 'don't' because Mrs. Thames had plunged the knife into his chest.

Directly into Melvin Cockburn's heart.

56

Melvin didn't realize he had been stabbed until he saw the look on Mrs. Thames's face. Her nostrils flared wide, her eyes opened wider, her mouth the widest of the set.

It was a look that spoke of shock, horror. It said that she had not meant to do what she had clearly meant to do. That she had needed him dead but had not wanted to do the killing.

And now there they were, both laying on the ground, different but the same.

Murderer and victim.

Murderer and victim.

Melvin was in shock as his body registered what had happen to him. He could see the knife standing stiffly from his chest, jutting straight out. It wasn't lodged in any bone but was deep in his heart. A heart he knew wasn't pure.

He felt a brief burst of pain shooting through every part of him. Felt it in his veins, as though his blood had turned to fire. Then the pain began to diminish, as did his life.

Melvin lay there leaking from the chest, Mrs. Thames lay there watching him do so, each drop of blood bringing her a step closer to becoming a confirmed killer.

He tried to talk, attempted to apologize, but the knife might as well have been plunged into his larynx, because he could not project the words.

It's okay, he wanted to tell her. It's okay. It was over now, he knew. And somehow, he was fine with that.

Now that he was dying, he could see things for what they were. He knew that Mrs. Thames had been telling the truth. He understood then what he had done. And understood that death was likely his best option based on what had become of his life. And what had become of his cat.

Lucy was dead. Her body was rotting on the kitchen table swarmed by flies and other creatures. What was the point of being alive now that the truth had become clear to him? Killing Mrs. Thames would have been a mistake. Killing all of them had been a mistake.

Well, maybe except for his mom.

On TV, in the movies, when someone is about to die their life flashes before their eyes. Melvin had always wondered if that was true. Now, with his life pouring out of him, he was surprised to find that it was. Partially. A portion of his life flashed before him like a bolt of lightning in an elsewise clear night sky. It was a flash of the last week and a half exclusively, starting with the day he had come back from the animal clinic after arguing with the veterinarian's assistant.

The day Lucy had died.

He didn't know exactly when it had happened, but after he had tripped in front of the Gormans' house, and checked to see if Lucy was okay, she had already been gone. It was a death he had so strongly denied that his conscious mind had not allowed him to acknowledge it.

He now recalled being on his cold basement floor, attempting to feed a broken-backed mouse to a cat that had been dead for hours, desperate to revive it. In that desperation, wanting to demonstrate how to eat the mouse like a parent eating a spoonful of baby food to encourage their toddler to follow suit, he had brought the mouse to his mouth. Then he had bitten into its underbelly, chewed its innards, including its still beating heart.

He now clearly remembered offering his mother's heart to his days-dead feline family as Lucy's corpse lay upon the kitchen table. He had poked her little nose and mouth repeatedly with the bloody organ before biting into the heart himself. Chewing, swallowing, vomiting it all up later. It had been the same with Brian.

He could see now why the people on the bus, in the mall, the waitress at the coffee shop, had all given him strange looks. It wasn't often you saw a man carrying around a dead cat everywhere he went.

He recalled why the cavity that had been made in the chest of Mrs. Gorman had been the size of his head. It was because he had pried apart her ribs, stuck his head inside of her as far as it could go until he found her heart, convincing himself, as he had done with the others, that it was still beating in her chest. Then he had bit and chewed long after she was dead, believing he was Lucy as he feasted on a human organ. All of this with Lucy's corpse on the bed beside them.

He also remembered what he had done with Mrs. Gorman's body afterward.

It had been tender. It had been intimate.

He remembered the monster he had become. And he remembered wanting, *needing* to be someone else. Anyone else. He had turned into his mother for a night, wearing her robe and slippers. He had put on Daniel Gorman's attire and had assumed the dead man's personality as well. All so he could run away from himself, and from this reality that had finally chased him down and caught him.

He had lost his mind, and so many people had lost their lives because of that. For all of this, and more, he wanted to apologize. But he couldn't. He didn't have strength enough to say a word.

Mrs. Thames had no problem speaking, however. Which was what she did.

After spitting out something small and pink and fleshy, she looked Melvin directly in his dying eyes. The look of guilt over killing him was gone; it had been replaced with rage, resentment, and the always familiar look of disappointment that Melvin was accustomed to by now.

"Crazy motherfucker," she spat. "I hope you rot in Hell!" Then, careful not to further hurt her tender ankle, she rose, stood unbalanced as she tried to avoid placing weight on her injured appendage. Melvin watched from the floor as she hobbled away. He couldn't stop her. And now that he had accepted the truth, he wouldn't have stopped her if he could.

Lucy was dead. She was the pet of the Reaper now. He had nothing and no one to live for.

Look at her, surviving again, Melvin thought as he watched Mrs. Thames limp to the door. *Surviving the so-called Aztec Killer.*

Huitzilopochtli! he now remembered. That was the name of the Sun God the Aztecs had sacrificed their victims to. He felt a grim sense of satisfaction now that he recalled it, realizing it would be the last good feeling he would ever have.

Mrs. Thames only looked back when she had opened the door and was halfway through it. She was checking to make sure he wasn't chasing her, something he was incapable of doing.

They locked eyes for a moment, a split second. Then she was all the way out the door, and slammed it shut behind her.

57

The door was closed. On Melvin. On his life.

And he was okay with that. Okay with meeting an end to a journey that had been angst filled and arduous. Okay with peace. Finally.

He began to shut his eyes to the closed door.

Until he saw another door opening.

He didn't realize what it was right away. At first it was only the eight-shaped knob, hovering there in the air. Then it became something else, something more.

Red roots, red branches, the Blood Red Door.

When the impossible entranceway opened, he saw clouds of brilliant blue. Then a form within those clouds. It was the silhouette of a man holding something in his right hand. When the man stepped from the clouds, out of the doorway, Melvin saw that it was a person he recognized.

He was looking at a sharply but antiquatedly dressed man. A black suit over a black shirt. A red and black bowtie. Red framed glasses. A black hat. And from that hat, blazing bright at the side of it, a burning feather.

From his prone position, lying on the floor, Melvin looked in awe at this strange, smiling man with his burning red feather and his burning blue eyes. A man who should not have been there standing next to a door that should not have existed.

Melvin now remembered clearly this door and this man, and the deal he had brokered with him. But just in case he didn't recall, in the event he misremembered, The Pitchman raised the briefcase in his right hand until it was level with his chest. Then he tapped it repeatedly, a reminder of what was in it. Of the price Melvin had paid. The sound his finger made against the attaché was that of the ticking of a clock.

Your time, Mr. Cockburn. Your time.

And now, his time was up.

Melvin watched the mist clear from the Blood Red Door. He witnessed the Blue Abyss become something else. Something substantial. Something that would have made him scream if he could only muster the strength to do so. What he was looking at was his fate, and he did not want to meet it.

What Melvin Cockburn saw was torture.

Tortures.

Through the door, he looked into Hell itself. And what he saw was Bright Red Madness.

It was a canyon the size of planets, a universe of woe. A world where the sun had been murdered, and had bled out where it once had shone. In that bloody sky were clouds of ash, and from them rained down fire.

The raining fire pooled, and those within it swam, magma making them move their bodies, pain their dance partner in this disco of the damned.

They shook, they squirmed, they screamed up at the scarlet sky. Melvin could hear them all, could hear them each. Uncountable souls, uncountable throats. From all of them, one voice. A voice that wailed, that bellowed its anguish, that cried for all to end. And as he looked into the Blood Red Door through heat-singed and teary eyes, Melvin saw that, for many of these people who were burning, melting, tortured, all did end. If an end can be a temporary thing.

Their skin bubbled, sloughed from their frames, the muscle beneath it burned down to bones. Bones roasted to cinders. And wherever their remains fell into the liquid fire, these tortured souls were reborn. To burn and cry and die again. And again. Ad infinitum.

As disturbing as the pools of fire seemed, things were somehow worse on the land surrounding them. On the beaches of black ash, the charcoal shores, the onyx mountains that touched the sun-bled sky.

On one of these mountains, Melvin saw a man rolling a boulder upward, a red-veined black rock the size of a mountain itself. He witnessed this man nearly reach the top, only for the stone to roll back to the bottom. For him to start again.

There were pits full of acid, with bodies immersed within. And like those inside the fire, they were killed and born to die again. Others were rolled in shattered glass, bathed in alcohol straight after. Animals Melvin had never seen, and could not describe now that he had, roamed atop the hard black land, goring, raping, gnawing on any soul within their reach.

Amidst the surrealness of what he was seeing – the open torture, the pools of fire, the pits of glass and acid – there were pockets of disquieting reality that confused Melvin as much as they concerned him.

He saw a street that could have been any street in his own neighbourhood. Except, on this street, every house was the same house. And each of them was on fire. A man ran from one burning dwelling to the next in search of something Melvin knew he would never find.

There was a chef inside a freestanding kitchen among those tortured in this fiery canyon. A cutting board was in front of him, an ancient cast iron pot with its contents aboil was on the stove beside him. On the cutting board: fingers, an ear, an eye. The chef wept from the eye remaining in his head as he prepared a meal made of himself.

Not far from the chef, but an eternity away, a man walked around an empty office in a suit made out of gnats, being eaten alive, howling as he wandered.

And, somehow, more terrifying than each of the trillions of tortures he was privy to, Melvin saw his mother.

She was sitting naked at a table in a chair, both made of black ice. A bottle in front of her, a glass there as well. She was drinking something that was not wine, sipping it even as it was burning her inside, causing her to bleed from the mouth.

She didn't seem to mind too much, though. Her attention was focused on Melvin, even all the way from Hell. She was looking at him, waiting for him. Smiling. Her teeth and tongue stained red.

"Noooooooo!" he screamed wildly into his house, finally finding his voice. It was all that he could do. His legs would not listen as he begged them to stand and run. His heart would not heed him as he pled for it to stop bleeding, to continue to keep him alive, to stave off the inevitable eternity ahead of him.

He couldn't move. He could only cry and wail. Which is what Melvin Cockburn – the man who would forever be known as the Aztec Killer – did in his final moments.

Laying there, looking into an illogical door, into a world that existed purely for punishment, staring at his mother who awaited him within it, Melvin screamed and screamed and screamed until he died.

POST-MORTEM

The Man with the Burning Feather in His Hat closed the door after ushering the soul of Melvin Cockburn through it. He looked down at the soulless corpse that remained on the foyer floor.

"That's a shame." He tsked, tutted, clucked his tongue.

The Pitchman stepped over Melvin as he made his way toward the kitchen. He had no interest in Melvin's body, nor in that of his victim in the house or those buried in the yard. He had taken from them what he needed.

He strode the length of the hall with a grin on his face, impressed by the damage Melvin had been able to do in such a short time. It was a decent little yield, a harvest he could be happy with. One his Red Father would be pleased by.

Whistling, he stepped over the body of Detective Kelly, tread across the pool of blood, and stood by the kitchen table upon which lay the corpse of a cat named Lucy.

He recalled the words he had said to Melvin when they had first conversed: *A creature that inspires this much devotion from its owner must make for a mighty fine pet.* And he thought now that a creature that could inspire such carnage should indeed make for a fine pet. His. It had been too long since he'd had a little companion. What he wanted was a friend who could accompany he and the other Children of The Road as they walked their endless walks.

Looking down at the decaying cat, still smiling, The Pitchman said,

"Not to worry little Lucy, time's not up for you."

He reached up to his hat. Reached for the burning feather.

Removing it from his fedora, The Pitchman touched the feather to the dead body of the cat. To her heart, until a small fire began to burn there. Then he simply watched.

His hands clasped in anticipation, he witnessed a body that had been skin and patchy fur atop a pile of bones begin to thicken, grow plump, the flesh becoming fuller. He watched as the hair that was gone grew back, became luxuriant, turned from a listless yellow to the colour of The Pitchman's feather as the flame he had placed at her heart spread throughout her body.

Lucy's coat burned brilliant gold, orange, deep crimson, all entwined; her fur was windblown fire.

He smiled and clapped a single time as the cat stood and shook herself, welcoming this strange new life into her body, getting a sense of her newfound sentience. Lucy looked at The Pitchman with eyes which were now Abysmal Blue. The same colour as his.

"Shall we?" he said to his new companion.

Lucy purred in response.

"Good."

When he turned, the door was there, immediately behind him. When he opened it, the sight inside of the doorway caused his smile to widen. He never tired of this view.

Through the door he looked upon it.

The Road.

It was shaped like infinity, made of black ice with veins of red and blue running through it. The Road floated in a sea of stars, weaving its way through worlds. There were endless wisps of white travelling across it, like ground fog shifting in a morning breeze.

Souls, so many souls, more fortunate than those Melvin had witnessed. They were on their path, each heading for one of the countless doorways that lined The Road. They were on their way to other existences. From one life to the next.

Around The Road, from below it, billowed the cobalt clouds of the Blue Abyss. Lucy seemed to be impressed by it all, looking through the Blood Red Door in wonder, meowing her approval.

Together, The Pitchman and his new companion set upon Infinity Road to continue their ceaseless mission.

To walk the worlds.

To catalyze, cause chaos.

To roam.

To reap.

THANKS FOR READING!

My cat, Cat, was the best cat ever. I know everyone says that about their cat, but seriously, mine was. Or at least top ten. She was with me through so many ups and downs, literally right by my side through everything. In the summer of 2022, when she developed a tumour on her chest and I was told her days were numbered, it was tough to imagine life without her. And things haven't quite been the same since she's been gone.

She left me with the following: guilt over whether I had taken too long to decide it was time for her to be put to sleep, thirteen years of memories with a loyal and entertaining pet, and the idea for this book. Her death also helped me solve a problem that had been bothering me for about a decade.

A Cat Named Lucy was one of the first characters I ever wrote about. She and The Red Lady, a demoness gorgon who has appeared in a few stories of mine, were both in a novel I wrote way back in 2011/2012, before I knew I seriously wanted to be a writer. The novel is called Red Room, and will be released at some point in the distant future because it needs major revisions. Until then, many of my stories are building up to that book.

Red Room was the catalyst for much of what I am writing now. And while The Red Lady received a backstory (in my debut collection How To Make A Monster: The Loveliest Shade of Red), and I created and implemented other Children of The Road such as The Pitchman, The Hanging Child, and The Black Man in the White Trench Coat, I couldn't figure out anything for A Cat Named Lucy (other than a very brief appearance in my novel, Bug Spray: A Tale of ~~Love and~~ Madness) until the day I decided it was time for Cat to be put to sleep after she would no longer eat. That was when the idea for Melvin and his humane sacrifices popped into my head. It was as though my imagination knew I needed something to focus on other than inevitable grief.

Humane Sacrifice was a great distraction. It turned out to be the most fun I've had while writing and revising a story. I hope you had fun with it as well, gory and gross as it is. Humane Sacrifice also turned out to be a story that connects with several of my other books. You'll see what I mean once you turn the page.

Thank you for reading this twisted tale, and I hope you look forward to reuniting with some of these characters and learning more about the places described in Humane Sacrifice down The Road.

As always, thanks to my accomplices, Courtney Swank, Rosco Nischler, and Ally Strzembely. And my brother, Fred.

– Dimaro
February 25, 2023

If you would like to spend more time with The Pitchman, check out *The Fire On Memory Lane*

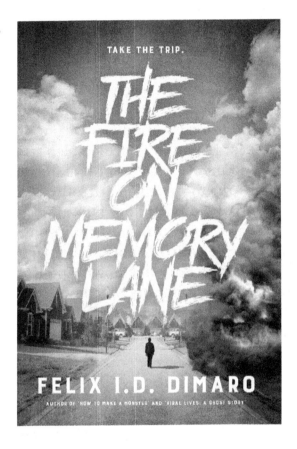

What would you pay to relive the best years of your life?

For Connor Michaels, recently divorced, alone, and grieving the death of his son, life doesn't seem worth living. All seems hopeless until he is offered a miracle solution to his malaise, a medicine that will allow him to block out the bad memories and relive the good ones in real time. At first it is salvation in a bottle, but Connor soon realizes that not every trip down Memory Lane is as blissful as it seems.

For more on Infinity Road, and The Children of The Road, check out How To Make A Monster: The Loveliest Shade of Red, and Bug Spray: A Tale of Madness

How To Make A Monster: A man wakes up in a jail cell with no memory of how he got there and no one to let him out, a chef is willing to sell his soul for the recipe for success, a drug addicted stripper has an accident at work and must face her past demons head on... How To Make A Monster explores the thin line between humanity and monstrosity which exists inside us all. Containing eight stories, this collection details how one wrong turn, one ill-timed hello, a goodbye that was planned too late, how any step we take can lead us down the path to monstrosity.

Bug Spray: A Tale of ~~Love and~~ Madness: Tybalt Ward is a boss. Young, good looking, ambitious, he is headed to the top and willing to leave behind broken hearts and broken lives along the way. The world is his until he meets someone who turns his world upside down. And Tybalt begins to learn that love and madness are two sides of the same coin.

Care to revisit Saturn City? Take another trip there by reading *The Corruption of Philip Toles* and *Viral Lives: A Ghost Story*

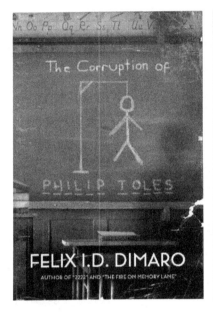 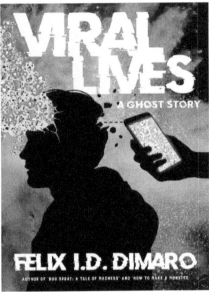

The Corruption of Philip Toles: On his thirteenth birthday, Philip Toles is found dead, hanging by the neck from the basketball rim of his school's gymnasium. A note is found on him indicating that a teacher was responsible for driving him to his end. But justice is never served, and Philip is quickly forgotten... Until thirteen years later, on the anniversary of his death, someone, or something, remembers Philip. And they are no longer interested in justice, because vengeance is being sought.

Viral Lives: A Ghost Story: Simon Hinch is a Gore Reporter. He spends late nights in bad places hoping to record violence for a fee. When Simon stumbles upon a man, bloody and dying in the street, he decides to film him instead of help. His footage is a viral sensation, and life is good for Simon. But it turns out that he may not have only captured a man's death on his phone, he may have captured a dead man's soul.

Take a walk into the Blue Abyss and travel to a desolate and desperate future in the time travel thriller 2222

The year is 2222, an ongoing population crisis has led to food and land shortages worldwide, and the creation of Satellite Cities - manmade islands full of sky-high slums. An extremist Neo-Nazi terrorist group has vowed to cut the world's population in half using a weapon buried by the Nazis during World War II
To stop them, a revolutionary scientist has found a way to go back in time and bring forward the weapon's creator, the only person who can stop inevitable doom. But will bringing forward one of the cruelest monsters from the past help save the future? Or will it prove to be a huge mistake? Only time will tell...

The Pitchman Will Return

Lucy Will Return

Stay updated on Dimaro's latest news and releases at
www.ThingsThatKeepMeUpAtNight.com and
substack.com/thingsthatkeepmeupatnight. Follow Dimaro on social
media: Instagram: @thingsthatkeepmeupatnight
Facebook: facebook.com/thingsthatkeepmeup and Slasher: @Dimaro

For Cat, A Eulogy

It was my ex-girlfriend's idea to get a cat. Our co-worker's cat had delivered a litter of kittens around Christmastime, and she was giving them away. When we went to see them, most of the kittens were on the couch being cuddly and cute, playing with the little humans there. But one of the kittens, clearly a bit of an asshole, was busy climbing up the Christmas tree. Without having to think it over, I said, "I want that one."

She never did become a cuddly cat. Didn't like being held or lifted up, hated to be placed on anyone's lap. But she made up for that over the next thirteen years by waiting for me at the door when I got home, obeying simple commands, eagerly following me wherever I went, and, whenever she could, she would lay right next to me, as close as she could be. That seemed to be her favourite spot.

When it came time to put her down after struggling with a massive chest tumour for months, I expected her to make a fuss. But she didn't. While I was sitting in the vet's office, in the room where pets are permanently put to sleep, she lay by my side and placed her head on my lap. And she died that way, in her favourite spot. Right next to me, as close as she could be.

RIP Chloe "Cat" Dimaro.

Made in the USA
Las Vegas, NV
26 April 2023

71120656R00134